The Little Prince

The Little Prince

小王子

——作者—安東尼・聖艾修伯里（Antoine de Saint-Exupéry）
——英譯者——（Katherine Woods）
——譯者—李思

CONTENTS

Part One

The Little Prince

Once when I was six years old I saw a magnificent picture in a book, called *True Stories from Nature*, about the primeval forest. It was a picture of a boa constrictor in the act of swallowing an animal. Here is a copy of the drawing.

In the book it said: "Boa constrictors swallow their prey whole, without chewing it. After that they are not able to move, and they sleep through the six months that they need for digestion."

I pondered deeply, then, over the adventures of the jungle. And after some work with a colored pencil I succeeded in making my first drawing. My Drawing Number One. It looked like this:

I showed my masterpiece to the grown-ups, and asked them whether the drawing frightened them.

But they answered: "Frighten? Why should any one be frightened by a hat?"

My drawing was not a picture of a hat. It was a picture of a boa constrictor digesting an elephant. But since the grown-ups were not able to understand it, I made another drawing: I drew the inside of the boa constrictor, so that the grown-ups could see it clearly. They always need to have things explained. My Drawing Number Two looked like this:

The grown-ups response, this time, was to advise me to lay aside my drawings of boa constrictors, whether from the inside or the outside and devote myself instead to geography, history, arithmetic and grammar. That is why, at the age of six, I gave up what might have been a magnificent career as a painter. I had been disheartened by the failure of my Drawing Number One and my Drawing Number Two. Grown-ups never understand anything by themselves, and it is tiresome for children to be always and forever explaining things to them.

So then I chose another profession, and learned to pilot airplanes. I have flown a little over all parts of the world; and it is true that geography has been very useful to me. At a glance I can distinguish China from Arizona. If one gets lost in the night, such knowledge is valuable.

In the course of this life I have had a great many encounters with a great many people who have been concerned with matters of consequence. I have lived a great deal among grown-ups. I have seen them intimately, close at hand. And that hasn't much improved my opinion of them.

Whenever I met one of them who seemed to me at all clear-sighted, I tried the experiment of showing him

my Drawing Number One, which I have always kept. I would try to find out, so, if this was a person of true understanding. But, whoever it was, he, or she, would always say:

"That is a hat."

Then I would never talk to that person about boa constrictors, or primeval forests, or stars. I would bring myself down to his level. I would talk to him about bridge, and golf, and politics, and neckties. And the grown-up would be greatly pleased to have met such a sensible man.

2 🪐

So I lived my life alone, without anyone that I could really talk to, until I had an accident with my plane in the Desert of Sahara, six years ago. Something was broken in my engine. And as I had with me neither a mechanic nor any passengers, I set myself to attempt the difficult repairs all alone. It was a question of life or death for me: I had scarcely enough drinking water to last a week.

The first night, then, I went to sleep on the sand, a thousand miles from any human habitation. I was more isolated than a shipwrecked sailor on a raft in the middle of the ocean. Thus you can imagine my amazement, at sunrise, when I was awakened by an odd little voice. It said:

"If you please—draw me a sheep!"

"What!"

"Draw me a sheep!"

Here you may see the best portrait that, later,
I was able to make of him.

I jumped to my feet, completely thunderstruck. I blinked my eyes hard. I looked carefully all around me. And I saw a most extraordinary small person, who stood there examining me with great seriousness. Here you may see the best portrait that, later, I was able to make of him. But my drawing is certainly very much less charming than its model.

That, however, is not my fault. The grown-ups discouraged me in my painter's career when I was six years old, and I never learned to draw anything, except boas from the outside and boas from the inside.

Now I stared at this sudden apparition with my eyes fairly starting out of my head in astonishment. Remember, I had crashed in the desert a thousand miles from any inhabited region. And yet my little man seemed neither to be straying uncertainly among the sands, nor to be fainting from fatigue or hunger or thirst or fear. Nothing about him gave any suggestion of a child lost in the middle of the desert, a thousand miles from any human habitation. When at last I was able to speak, I said to him:

"But—what are you doing here?"

And in answer he repeated, very slowly, as if he were speaking of a matter of great consequence:

"If you please—draw me a sheep…"

When a mystery is too overpowering, one dare not disobey. Absurd as it might seem to me, a thousand miles from any human habitation and in danger of death, I took out of my pocket a sheet of paper and my fountain pen. But then I remembered how my studies had been concentrated on geography, history, arithmetic and grammar, and I told the little chap (a little crossly, too) that I did not know how to draw. He answered me:

"That doesn't matter. Draw me a sheep…"

But I had never drawn a sheep. So I drew for him one of the two pictures I had drawn so often. It was that of the boa constrictor from the outside. And I was astounded to hear the little fellow greet it with:

"No, no, no! I do not want an elephant inside a boa constrictor. A boa constrictor is a very dangerous creature, and an elephant is very cumbersome. Where

I live, everything is very small. What I need is a sheep.
Draw me a sheep."

So then I made a drawing.

He looked at it carefully, then
he said:

"No. This sheep is already very
sickly. Make me another."

So I made another drawing.

My friend smiled gently and
indulgently.

"You see yourself," he said," that this is not a sheep.
This is a ram. It has horns."

So then I did my drawing over once
more.

But it was rejected too, just like the
others.

"This one is too old. I want a sheep
that will live a long time."

By this time my patience was
exhausted, because I was in a hurry to start taking my
engine apart. So I tossed off this drawing. And I threw
out an explanation with it.

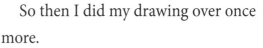

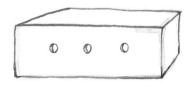

"This is only his box. The sheep you asked for is inside."

I was very surprised to see a light break over the face of my young judge:

"That is exactly the way I wanted it! Do you think that this sheep will have to have a great deal of grass?"

"Why?"

"Because where I live everything is very small…"

"There will surely be enough grass for him," I said. "It is a very small sheep that I have given you."

He bent his head over the drawing:

"Not so small that—Look! He has gone to sleep…"

And that is how I made the acquaintance of the little prince.

3 🪐

🎧 3

It took me a long time to learn where he came from. The little prince, who asked me so many questions, never seemed to hear the ones I asked him. It was from words dropped by chance that, little by little, everything was revealed to me.

The first time he saw my airplane, for instance (I shall not draw my airplane; that would be much too complicated for me), he asked me:

"What is that object?"

"That is not an object. It flies. It is an airplane. It is my airplane."

And I was proud to have him learn that I could fly.

He cried out, then:

"What! You dropped down from the sky?"

"Yes," I answered, modestly.

"Oh! That is funny!"

And the little prince broke into a lovely peal of laughter, which irritated me very much. I like my misfortunes to be taken seriously.

Then he added:

"So you, too, come from the sky! Which is your planet?"

At that moment I caught a gleam of light in the impenetrable mystery of his presence; and I demanded, abruptly:

"Do you come from another planet?"

But he did not reply. He tossed his head gently, without taking his eyes from my plane.

"It is true that on that you can't have come from very far away…"

And he sank into a reverie, which lasted a long time. Then, taking my sheep out of his pocket, he buried himself in the contemplation of his treasure.

You can imagine how my curiosity was aroused by

this half confidence about the "other planets." I made a great effort, therefore, to find out more on this subject.

"My little man, where do you come from? What is this where I live, of which you speak? Where do you want to take your sheep?"

After a reflective silence he answered:

"The thing that is so good about the box you have given me is that at night he can use it as his house."

"That is so. And if you are good I will give you a string, too, so that you can tie him during the day, and a post to tie him to."

But the little prince seemed shocked by this offer:

"Tie him! What a queer idea!"

"But if you don't tie him," I said, "he will wander off somewhere, and get lost."

My friend broke into another peal of laughter:

"But where do you think he would go?"

"Anywhere. Straight ahead of him."

Then the little prince said, earnestly:

"That doesn't matter. Where I live, everything is so small!"

And, with perhaps a hint of sadness, he added:

"Straight ahead of him, nobody can go very far..."

4

I had thus learned a second fact of great importance: this was that the planet the little prince came from was scarcely any larger than a house!

But that did not really surprise me much. I knew very well that in addition to the great planets—such as the Earth, Jupiter, Mars, Venus—to which we have given names, there are also hundreds of others, some of which are so small that one has a hard time seeing them through the telescope. When an astronomer discovers one of these he does not give it a name, but only a number. He might call it, for example, "Asteroid 325."

I have serious reason to believe that the planet from which the little prince came is the asteroid known as B-612.

This asteroid has only once been seen through the telescope. That was by a Turkish astronomer, in 1909.

On making his discovery, the astronomer had presented it to the International Astronomical Congress, in a great demonstration. But he was in Turkish

The Little Prince on Asteroid B-612

costume, and so nobody would believe what he said.

Grown-ups are like that…

Fortunately, however, for the reputation of Asteroid B-612, a Turkish dictator made a law that his subjects, under pain of death, should change to European costume. So in 1920 the astronomer gave his demonstration all over again, dressed with impressive style and elegance. And this time everybody accepted his report.

If I have told you these details about the asteroid, and made a note of its number for you, it is on account of the grown-ups and their ways. Grown-ups love figures. When you tell them that you have made a new friend, they never ask you any questions about essential matters. They never say to you, "What does his voice sound like? What games does he love best? Does he collect butterflies?" Instead, they demand: "How old is he? How many brothers has he? How much does he weigh? How much money does his father make?"

Only from these figures do they think they have learned anything about him.

If you were to say to the grown-ups: "I saw a beautiful house made of rosy brick, with geraniums in the windows and doves on the roof," they would not be able to get any idea of that house at all. You would have to say to them: "I saw a house that cost $20,000." Then they would exclaim: "Oh, what a pretty house that is!"

Just so, you might say to them: "The proof that the little prince existed is that he was charming, that he laughed, and that he was looking for a sheep. If anybody wants a sheep, that is a proof that he exists." And what good would it do to tell them that? They would shrug their shoulders, and treat you like a child. But if you said

to them: "The planet he came from is Asteroid B-612," then they would be convinced, and leave you in peace from their questions.

They are like that. One must not hold it against them. Children should always show great forbearance toward grown-up people.

But certainly, for us who understand life, figures are a matter of indifference. I should have liked to begin this story in the fashion of the fairy-tales. I should have liked to say: "Once upon a time there was a little prince who lived on a planet that was scarcely any bigger than himself, and who had need of a sheep…"

To those who understand life, that would have given a much greater air of truth to my story.

For I do not want anyone to read my book carelessly. I have suffered too much grief in setting down these memories. Six years have already passed since my friend went away from me, with his sheep. If I try to describe him here, it is to make sure that I shall not forget him. To forget a friend is sad. Not everyone has had a friend. And if I forget him, I may become like the grown-ups who are no longer interested in anything but figures…

It is for that purpose, again, that I have bought a box

of paints and some pencils. It is hard to take up drawing again at my age, when I have never made any pictures except those of the boa constrictor from the outside and the boa constrictor from the inside, since I was six. I shall certainly try to make my portraits as true to life as possible. But I am not at all sure of success. One drawing goes along all right, and another has no resemblance to its subject. I make some errors, too, in the little prince's height: in one place he is too tall and in another too short. And I feel some doubts about the color of his costume. So I fumble along as best I can, now good, now

bad, and I hope generally fair-to-middling.

In certain more important details I shall make mistakes, also. But that is something that will not be my fault. My friend never explained anything to me. He thought, perhaps, that I was-like himself. But I, alas, do not know how to see sheep through the walls of boxes. Perhaps I am a little like the grown-ups. I have had to grow old.

5 🪐

As each day passed I would learn, in our talk, something about the little prince's planet, his departure from it, his journey. The information would come very slowly, as it might chance to fall from his thoughts. It was in this way that I heard, on the third day, about the catastrophe of the baobabs.

This time, once more, I had the sheep to thank for it. For the little prince asked me abruptly—as if seized by a grave doubt—"It is true, isn't it, that sheep eat little bushes?"

"Yes, that is true."

"Ah! I am glad!"

I did not understand why it was so important that sheep should eat little bushes. But the little prince added:

"Then it follows that they also eat baobabs?"

I pointed out to the little prince that baobabs were not little bushes, but, on the contrary, trees as big as castles; and that even if he took a whole herd of elephants away

with him, the herd would
not eat up one single
baobab.

The idea of the herd of
elephants made the little
prince laugh.

"We would have to put
them one on top of the
other," he said.

But he made a wise
comment:

"Before they grow so big, the baobabs start out by
being little."

"That is strictly correct," I said. "But why do you want
the sheep to eat the little baobabs?"

He answered me at once, "Oh, come, come!", as if he
were speaking of something that was self-evident. And
I was obliged to make a great mental effort to solve this
problem, without any assistance.

Indeed, as I learned, there were on the planet where
the little prince lived—as on all planets—good plants
and bad plants. In consequence, there were good seeds
from good plants, and bad seeds from bad plants. But

seeds are invisible. They sleep deep in the heart of the
earth's darkness, until someone among them is seized
with the desire to awaken. Then this little seed will
stretch itself and begin—timidly at first—to push a
charming little sprig inoffensively upward toward the
sun. If it is only a sprout of radish or the sprig of a rose-
bush, one would let it grow wherever it might wish. But
when it is a bad plant, one must destroy it as soon as
possible, the very first instant that one recognizes it.

Now there were some terrible seeds on the planet that was the home of the little prince; and these were the seeds of the baobab.

The soil of that planet was infested with them. A baobab is something you will never, never be able to get rid of if you attend to it too late. It spreads over the entire planet. It bores clear through it with its roots. And if the planet is too small, and the baobabs are too many, they split it in pieces…

"It is a question of discipline," the little prince said to me later on. "When you've finished your own toilet in the morning, then it is time to attend to the toilet of your planet, just so, with the greatest care. You must see to it that you pull up regularly all the baobabs, at the very first moment when they can be distinguished from the rose-bushes which they resemble so closely in their earliest youth. It is very tedious work," the little prince added, "but very easy."

And one day he said to me: "You ought to make a beautiful drawing, so that the children where you live can see exactly how all this is. That would be very useful to them if they were to travel some day. Sometimes," he added, "there is no harm in putting off a piece of work

The Baobabs

until another day. But when it is a matter of baobabs, that always means a catastrophe. I knew a planet that was inhabited by a lazy man. He neglected three little bushes…"

So, as the little prince described it to me, I have made a drawing of that planet. I do not much like to take the tone of a moralist. But the danger of the baobabs is so little understood, and such considerable risks would be run by anyone who might get lost on an asteroid, that for once I am breaking through my reserve. "Children," I say plainly, "watch out for the baobabs."

My friends, like myself, have been skirting this danger for a long time, without ever knowing it; and so it is for them that I have worked so hard over this drawing. The lesson which I pass on by this means is worth all the trouble it has cost me.

Perhaps you will ask me, "Why are there no other drawings in this book as magnificent and impressive as this drawing of the baobabs?"

The reply is simple. I tried. But with the others I have not been successful. When I made the drawing of the baobabs I was carried beyond myself by the inspiring force of urgent necessity.

6

Oh, little prince! Bit by bit I came to understand the secrets of your sad little life… For a long time you had found your only entertainment in the quiet pleasure of looking at the sunset. I learned that new detail on the morning of the fourth day, when you said to me:

"I am very fond of sunsets. Come, let us go look at a sunset now."

"But we must wait," I said.

"Wait? For what?"

"For the sunset. We must wait until it is time."

At first you seemed to be very much surprised. And then you laughed to yourself. You said to me:

"I am always thinking that I am at home."

Just so. Everybody knows that when it is noon in the United States the sun is setting over France. If you could fly to France in one minute, you could go straight into the sunset, right from noon. Unfortunately, France is too far away for that. But on your tiny planet, my little prince, all you need to do is move your chair a few steps.

You can see the day end and the twilight falling whenever you like…

"One day," you said to me:

"I saw the sunset forty-four times!"

And a little later you added:

"You know—one loves the sunset, when one is so sad…"

"Were you so sad, then?" I asked, "on the day of the forty-four sunsets?"

But the little prince made no reply.

7 🪐

🎧 7

On the fifth day—again, as always, it was thanks to the sheep—the secret of the little prince's life was revealed to me. Abruptly, without anything to lead up to it, and as if the question had been born of long and silent meditation on his problem, he demanded:

"A sheep—if it eats little bushes, does it eat flowers, too?"

"A sheep," I answered, "eats anything it finds in its reach."

"Even flowers that have thorns?"

"Yes, even flowers that have thorns."

"Then the thorns—what use are they?"

I did not know. At that moment I was very busy trying to unscrew a bolt that had got stuck in my engine. I was very much worried, for it was becoming clear to me that the breakdown of my plane was extremely serious. And I had so little drinking water left that I had to fear the worst.

"The thorns—what use are they?"

The little prince never let go of a question, once he had asked it. As for me, I was upset over that bolt. And I answered with the first thing that came into my head:

"The thorns are of no use at all. Flowers have thorns just for spite!"

"Oh!"

There was a moment of complete silence. Then the little prince flashed back at me, with a kind of resentfulness:

"I don't believe you! Flowers are weak creatures. They are naive. They reassure themselves as best they can. They believe that their thorns are terrible weapons..."

I did not answer. At this instant I was saying to myself: "If this bolt still won't turn, I am going to knock it out with the hammer." Again the little prince disturbed my thoughts:

"And you actually believe that the flowers—"

"Oh, no!" I cried. "No, no, no! I don't believe anything. I answered you with the first thing that came into my head. Don't you see—I am very busy with matters of consequence!"

He stared at me, thunderstruck.

"Matters of consequence!"

He looked at me there, with my hammer in my hand, my fingers black with engine-grease, bending down over an object which seemed to him extremely ugly...

"You talk just like the grown-ups!"

That made me a little ashamed. But he went on, relentlessly:

"You mix everything up together... You confuse everything..."

He was really very angry. He tossed his golden curls in the breeze.

"I know a planet where there is a certain red-faced gentleman. He has never smelled a flower. He has never looked at a star. He has never loved any one. He has never done anything in his life but add up figures. And all day he says over and over, just like you: 'I am busy with matters of consequence!' And that makes him swell up with pride. But he is not a man—he is a mushroom!"

"A what?"

"A mushroom!"

The little prince was now white with rage.

"The flowers have been growing thorns for millions of years. For millions of years the sheep have been eating them just the same. And is it not a matter of consequence to try to understand why the flowers go to so much trouble to grow thorns which are never of any use to them? Is the warfare between the sheep and the flowers not important? Is this not of more consequence than a fat red-faced gentleman's sums? And if I know—I, myself—one flower which is unique in the world, which grows nowhere but on my planet, but which one little sheep can destroy in a single bite some morning, without even noticing what he is doing—Oh! You think that is not important!"

His face turned from white to red as he continued:

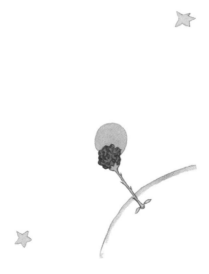

"If someone loves a flower, of which just one single blossom grows in all the millions and millions of stars, it is enough to make him happy just to look at the stars. He can say to himself: 'Somewhere, my flower is there…' But if the sheep eats the flower, in one moment all his stars will be darkened… And you think that is not important!"

He could not say anything more. His words were choked by sobbing.

The night had fallen. I had let my tools drop from my hands. Of what moment now was my hammer, my bolt, or thirst, or death? On one star, one planet, my planet, the Earth, there was a little prince to be comforted. I took him in my arms, and rocked him. I said to him:

"The flower that you love is not in danger. I will draw you a muzzle for your sheep. I will draw you a railing to put around your flower. I will—"

I did not know what to say to him. I felt awkward and blundering. I did not know how I could reach him, where I could overtake him and go on hand in hand with him once more.

It is such a secret place, the land of tears.

8 🪐

🎧 8

I soon learned to know this flower better. On the little prince's planet the flowers had always been very simple. They had only one ring of petals; they took up no room at all; they were a trouble to nobody. One morning they would appear in the grass, and by night they would have faded peacefully away. But one day, from a seed blown from no one knew where, a new flower had come up; and the little prince had watched very closely over this small sprout which was not like any other small sprouts on his planet. It might, you see, have been a new kind of baobab.

But the shrub soon stopped growing, and began to get ready to produce a flower. The little prince, who was present at the first appearance of a huge bud, felt at once

that some sort of miraculous apparition must emerge from it. But the flower was not satisfied to complete the preparations for her beauty in the shelter of her green chamber. She chose her colors with the greatest care. She dressed herself slowly. She adjusted her petals one by one. She did not wish to go out into the world all rumpled, like the field poppies. It was only in the full radiance of her beauty that she wished to appear. Oh, yes! She was a coquettish creature! And her mysterious adornment lasted for days and days.

Then one morning, exactly at sunrise, she suddenly showed herself.

And, after working with all this painstaking precision, she yawned and said:

"Ah! I am scarcely awake. I beg that you will excuse me. My petals are still all disarranged…"

But the little prince could not restrain his admiration:

"Oh! How beautiful you are!"

"Am I not?" the flower responded, sweetly. "And I was born at the same moment as the sun…"

The little prince could guess easily enough that she was not any too modest—but how moving—and exciting—she was!

"I think it is time for breakfast," she added an instant later. "If you would have the kindness to think of my needs—"

And the little prince, completely abashed, went to look for a sprinkling-can of fresh water. So, he tended the flower.

So, too, she began very quickly to torment him with her vanity—which was, if the truth be known, a little difficult to deal with. One day, for instance, when she was speaking of her four thorns, she said to the little prince:

"Let the tigers come with their claws!"

"There are no tigers on my planet," the little prince objected. "And, anyway, tigers do not eat weeds."

"I am not a weed," the flower replied, sweetly.

"Please excuse me…"

"I am not at all afraid of tigers," she went on. "But I have a horror of drafts. I suppose you wouldn't have a screen for me?"

"A horror of drafts—that is bad luck, for a plant," remarked the little prince, and added to himself, "This flower is a very complex creature…"

"At night I want you to put me under a glass globe. It is very cold where you live. In the place I came from—"

But she interrupted herself at that point. She had come in the form of a seed. She could not have known anything of any other worlds. Embarrassed over having let herself be caught on the verge of such a naive untruth, she coughed two or three times, in order to put the little prince in the wrong.

"The screen?"

"I was just going to look for it when you spoke to me…"

Then she forced her cough a little more so that he should suffer

from remorse just the same.

So the little prince, in spite of all the good will that was inseparable from his love, had soon come to doubt her. He had taken seriously words which were without importance, and it made him very unhappy.

"I ought not to have listened to her," he confided to me one day. "One never ought to listen to the flowers. One should simply look at them and breathe their fragrance. Mine perfumed all my planet. But I did not know how to take pleasure in all her grace. This tale of claws, which disturbed me so much, should only have filled my heart with tenderness and pity."

And he continued his confidences:

"The fact is that I did not know how to understand anything! I ought to have judged by deeds and not by words. She cast her fragrance and her radiance over me. I ought never to have run away from her... I ought to have guessed all the affection that lay behind her poor little stratagems. Flowers are so inconsistent! But I was too young to know how to love her..."

9 🪐

I believe that for his escape he took advantage of the migration of a flock of wild birds. On the morning of his departure he put his planet in perfect order. He carefully cleaned out his active volcanoes. He possessed two active volcanoes; and they were very convenient for heating his breakfast in the morning. He also had one volcano that was extinct. But, as he said. "One never knows!" So he cleaned out the extinct volcano, too. If they are well cleaned out, volcanoes burn slowly and steadily, without any eruptions. Volcanic eruptions are like fires in a chimney.

On our Earth we are obviously much too small to clean out our volcanoes. That is why they bring no end of trouble upon us.

The little prince also pulled up, with a certain sense of dejection, the last little shoots of the baobabs. He believed that he would never want to return. But on this last morning all these familiar tasks seemed very precious to him. And when he watered the flower for the last

He carefully cleaned out
his active volcanoes.

time, and prepared to place her under the shelter of her glass globe, he realized that he was very close to tears.

"Goodbye," he said to the flower.

But she made no answer.

"Goodbye," he said again.

The flower coughed. But it was not because she had a cold.

"I have been silly," she said to him, at last. "I ask your forgiveness. Try to be happy…"

He was surprised by this absence of reproaches. He stood there all bewildered, the glass globe held arrested in mid-air. He did not understand this quiet sweetness.

"Of course I love you," the flower said to him. "It is my fault that you have not known it all the while. That is of no importance. But you—you have been just as foolish as I. Try to be happy... Let the glass globe be. I don't want it any more."

"But the wind—"

"My cold is not so bad as all that... The cool night air will do me good. I am a flower."

"But the animals—"

"Well, I must endure the presence of two or three caterpillars if I wish to become acquainted with the butterflies. It seems that they are very beautiful. And if not the butterflies—and the caterpillars—who will call upon me? You will be far away... As for the large animals—I am not at all afraid of any of them. I have my claws."

And, naïvely, she showed her four thorns. Then she added:

"Don't linger like this. You have decided to go away. Now go!"

For she did not want him to see her crying. She was such a proud flower...

10 🪐

🎧 10

He found himself in the neighborhood of the asteroids 325, 326, 327, 328, 329, and 330. He began, therefore, by visiting them, in order to add to his knowledge.

The first of them was inhabited by a king. Clad in royal purple and ermine, he was seated upon a throne which was at the same time both simple and majestic.

"Ah! Here is a subject," exclaimed the king, when he saw the little prince coming.

And the little prince asked himself:

"How could he recognize me when he had never seen me before?"

He did not know how the world is simplified for kings. To them, all men are subjects.

"Approach, so that I may see you better," said the king, who felt consumingly proud of being at last a king over somebody.

The little prince looked everywhere to find a place to sit down; but the entire planet was crammed and

obstructed by the king's magnificent ermine robe. So he remained standing upright, and, since he was tired, he yawned.

"It is contrary to etiquette to yawn in the presence of a king," the monarch said to him. "I forbid you to do so."

"I can't help it. I can't stop myself," replied the little prince, thoroughly embarrassed. "I have come on a long journey, and I have had no sleep…"

"Ah, then," the king said. "I order you to yawn. It is years since I have seen anyone yawning. Yawns, to me, are objects of curiosity. Come, now! Yawn again! It is an order."

"That frightens me…I cannot, any more…" murmured the little prince, now completely abashed.

"Hum! Hum!" replied the king. "Then I—I order you sometimes to yawn and sometimes to—"

He sputtered a little, and seemed vexed.

For what the king fundamentally insisted upon was that his authority should be respected. He tolerated no disobedience. He was an absolute monarch. But, because he was a very good man, he made his orders reasonable.

"If I ordered a general," he would say, by way of example, "if I ordered a general to change himself into a

sea bird, and if the general did not obey me, that would not be the fault of the general. It would be my fault."

"May I sit down?" came now a timid inquiry from the little prince.

"I order you to do so," the king answered him, and majestically gathered in a fold of his ermine mantle.

But the little prince was wondering… The planet was tiny. Over what could this king really rule?

"Sire," he said to him, "I beg that you will excuse my asking you a question—"

"I order you to ask me a question," the king hastened to assure him.

"Sire—over what do you rule?"

"Over everything," said the king, with magnificent simplicity.

"Over everything?"

The king made a gesture, which took in his planet, the other planets, and all the stars.

"Over all that?" asked the little prince.

"Over all that," the king answered.

For his rule was not only absolute, it was also universal.

"And the stars obey you?"

"Certainly they do," the king said. "They obey instantly. I do not permit insubordination."

Such power was a thing for the little prince to marvel at. If he had been master of such complete authority, he would have been able to watch the sunset, not forty-four times in one day, but seventy-two, or even a hundred, or even two hundred times, without ever having to move his chair. And because he felt a bit sad as he remembered his little planet which he had forsaken, he plucked up his courage to ask the king a favor:

"I should like to see a sunset... Do me that kindness... order the sun to set..."

"If I ordered a general to fly from one flower to another like a butterfly, or to write a tragic drama, or to change himself into a sea bird, and if the general did not carry out the order that he had received, which one of us would be in the wrong?" the king demanded. "The general, or myself?"

"You," said the little prince firmly.

"Exactly. One must require from each one the duty which each one can perform," the king went on. "Accepted authority rests first of all on reason. If you ordered your people to go and throw themselves into

the sea, they would rise up in revolution. I have the right to require obedience because my orders are reasonable."

"Then my sunset?" the little prince reminded him: for he never forgot a question once he had asked it.

"You shall have your sunset. I shall command it. But, according to my science of government, I shall wait until conditions are favorable."

"When will that be?" inquired the little prince.

"Hum! Hum!" replied the king; and before saying anything else he consulted a bulky almanac. "Hum! Hum! That will be about—about—that will be this evening about twenty minutes to eight. And you will see how well I am obeyed!"

The little prince yawned. He was regretting his lost sunset. And then, too, he was already beginning to be a little bored.

"I have nothing more to do here" he said to the king. "So I shall set out on my way again."

"Do not go," said the king, who was very proud of having a subject. "Do not go. I will make you a Minister!"

"Minister of what?"

"Minister of—of Justice!"

"But there is nobody here to judge!"

"We do not know that," the king said to him. "I have not yet made a complete tour of my kingdom. I am very old. There is no room here for a carriage. And it tires me to walk."

"Oh, but I have looked already!" said the little prince, turning around to give one more glance to the other side of the planet. On that side, as on this, there was nobody at all…

"Then you shall judge yourself," the king answered. "That is the most difficult thing of all. It is much more difficult to judge oneself than to judge others. If you succeed in judging yourself rightly, then you are indeed a man of true wisdom."

"Yes," said the little prince, "but I can judge myself anywhere. I do not need to live on this planet."

"Hum! Hum!" said the king. "I have good reason to believe that somewhere on my planet there is an old rat. I hear him at night. You can judge this old rat. From time to time you will condemn him to death. Thus his life will depend on your justice. But you will pardon him on each occasion; for he must be treated thriftily. He is the only one we have."

"I," replied the little prince, "do not like to condemn anyone to death. And now I think I will go on my way."

"No," said the king.

But the little prince, having now completed his preparations for departure, had no wish to grieve the old monarch.

"If Your Majesty wishes to be promptly obeyed," he said, "he should be able to give me a reasonable order. He should be able, for example, to order me to be gone by the end of one minute. It seems to me that conditions are favorable…"

As the king made no answer, the little prince hesitated a moment. Then, with a sigh, he took his leave.

"I make you my Ambassador," the king called out, hastily.

He had a magnificent air of authority.

"The grown-ups are very strange," the little prince said to himself, as he continued on his journey.

11

The second planet was inhabited by a conceited man.

"Ah! Ah! I am about to receive a visit from an admirer," he exclaimed from afar, when he first saw the little prince coming.

For, to conceited man, all other men are admirers.

"Good morning," said the little prince. "That is a queer hat you are wearing."

"It is a hat for salutes," the conceited man replied. "It is to raise in salute when people acclaim me. Unfortunately, nobody at all ever passes this way."

"Yes?" said the little prince, who did not understand what the conceited man was talking about.

"Clap your hands, one against the other," the conceited man now directed him.

The little prince clapped his hands. The conceited man raised his hat in a modest salute.

"This is more entertaining than the visit to the king," the little prince said to himself. And he began again to clap his hands, one against the other. The conceited man again raised his hat in salute.

After five minutes of this exercise the little prince grew tired of the game's monotony.

"And what should one do to make the hat come down?" he asked.

But the conceited man did not hear him. Conceited people never hear anything but praise.

"Do you really admire me very much?" he demanded of the little prince.

"What does that mean…'admire'?"

"To admire means that you regard me as the handsomest, the best-dressed, the richest, and the most intelligent man on this planet."

"But you are the only man on your planet!"

"Do me this kindness. Admire me just the same."

"I admire you," said the little prince, shrugging his shoulders slightly, "but what is there in that to interest you so much?"

And the little prince went away.

"The grown-ups are certainly very odd," he said to himself, as he continued on his journey.

12

The next planet was inhabited by a tippler. This was a very short visit, but it plunged the little prince into deep dejection.

"What are you doing there?" he said to the tippler, whom he found settled down in silence before a collection of empty bottles and also a collection of full bottles.

"I am drinking," replied the tippler, with a lugubrious air.

"Why are you drinking?" demanded the little prince.

"So that I may forget," replied the tippler.

"Forget what?" inquired the little prince, who already was sorry for him.

"Forget that I am ashamed," the tippler confessed, hanging his head.

"Ashamed of what?" insisted the little prince, who wanted to help him.

"Ashamed of drinking!" The tippler brought his speech to an end, and shut himself up in an impregnable silence.

And the little prince went away, puzzled.

"The grown-ups are certainly very, very odd," he said to himself, as he continued on his journey.

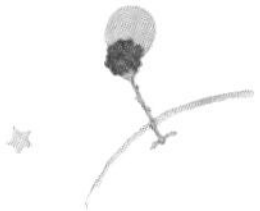

13

The fourth planet belonged to a businessman. This man was so much occupied that he did not even raise his head at the little prince's arrival.

"Good morning," the little prince said to him. "Your cigarette has gone out."

"Three and two make five. Five and seven make twelve. Twelve and three make fifteen. Good morning. Fifteen and seven make twenty-two. Twenty-two and six make twenty-eight. I haven't time to light it again. Twenty-six and five make thirty-one. Phew! Then that makes five-hundred-and-one million, six-hundred-twenty-two thousand, seven-hundred-thirty-one."

"Five hundred million what?" asked the little prince.

"Eh? Are you still there? Five-hundred-and-one million—I can't stop... I have so much to do! I am concerned with matters of consequence. I don't amuse myself with balderdash. Two and five make seven..."

"Five-hundred-and-one million what?" repeated the little prince, who never in his life had let go of a question once he had asked it.

The businessman raised his head.

"During the fifty-four years that I have inhabited this planet, I have been disturbed only three times. The first time was twenty-two years ago, when some giddy goose fell from goodness knows where. He made the most frightful noise that resounded all over the place, and I made four mistakes in my addition. The second time, eleven years ago, I was disturbed by an attack of rheumatism. I don't get enough exercise. I have no time for loafing. The third time—well, this is it! I was saying, then, five-hundred-and-one million—"

"Millions of what?"

The businessman suddenly realized that there was no hope of being left in peace until he answered this question.

"Millions of those little objects," he said, "which one sometimes sees in the sky."

"Flies?"

"Oh, no. Little glittering objects."

"Bees?"

"Oh, no. Little golden objects that set lazy men to idle dreaming. As for me, I am concerned with matters of consequence. There is no time for idle dreaming in my life."

"Ah! You mean the stars?"

"Yes, that's it. The stars."

"And what do you do with five-hundred million of stars?"

"Five-hundred-and-one million, six-hundred-twenty-two thousand, seven-hundred-thirty-one. I am concerned with matters of consequence. I am accurate."

"And what do you do with these stars?"

"What do I do with them?"

"Yes."

"Nothing. I own them."

"You own the stars?"

"Yes."

"But I have already seen a king who—"

"Kings do not own; they reign over. It is a very different matter."

"And what good does it do you to own the stars?"

"It does me the good of making me rich."

"And what good does it do you to be rich?"

"It makes it possible for me to buy more stars, if any are discovered."

"This man," the little prince said to himself, "reasons a little like my poor tippler…"

Nevertheless, he still had some more questions.

"How is it possible for one to own the stars?"

"To whom do they belong?" the businessman retorted, peevishly.

"I don't know. To nobody."

"Then they belong to me, because I was the first person to think of it."

"Is that all that is necessary?"

"Certainly. When you find a diamond that belongs to nobody, it is yours. When you discover an island that belongs to nobody, it is yours. When you get an idea before any one else, you take out a patent on it, it is yours. So with me, I own the stars, because nobody else before me ever thought of owning them."

"Yes, that is true," said the little prince. "And what do you do with them?"

"I administer them," replied the businessman. "I count them and recount them. It is difficult. But I am a man who is naturally interested in matters of consequence."

The little prince was still not satisfied.

"If I owned a silk scarf," he said, "I could put it around my neck and take it away with me. If I owned a flower, I could pluck that flower and take it away with me. But

you cannot pluck the stars from heaven…"

"No. But I can put them in the bank."

"Whatever does that mean?"

"That means that I write the number of my stars on a little paper. And then I put this paper in a drawer and lock it with a key."

"And that is all?"

"That is enough," said the businessman.

"It is entertaining," thought the little prince. "It is rather poetic. But it is of no great consequence."

On matters of consequence, the little prince had ideas which were very different from those of the grown-ups.

"I myself own a flower," he continued his conversation with the businessman, "which I water every day. I own three volcanoes, which I clean out every week (for I also clean out the one that is extinct; one never knows). It is of some use to my volcanoes, and it is of some use to my flower, that I own them. But you are of no use to the stars…"

The businessman opened his mouth, but he found nothing to say in answer. And the little prince went away.

"The grown-ups are certainly altogether extraordinary," he said simply, talking to himself as he continued on his journey.

14 🪐

The fifth planet was very strange. It was the smallest of all. There was just enough room on it for a street lamp and a lamplighter. The little prince was not able to reach any explanation of the use of a street lamp and a lamplighter, somewhere in the heavens, on a planet which had no people, and not one house. But he said to himself, nevertheless:

"It may well be that this man is absurd. But he is not so absurd as the king, the conceited man, the businessman, and the tippler. For at least his work has some meaning. When he lights his street lamp, it is as if he brought one more star to life, or one flower. When he puts out his lamp, he sends the flower, or the star, to sleep. That is a beautiful occupation. And since it is beautiful, it is truly useful."

When he arrived on the planet he respectfully saluted the lamplighter.

"Good morning. Why have you just put out your lamp?"

I follow a terrible profession.

"Those are the orders," replied the lamplighter. "Good morning."

"What are the orders?"

"The orders are that I put out my lamp. Good evening."

And he lighted his lamp again.

"But why have you just lighted it again?"

"Those are the orders," replied the lamplighter.

"I do not understand," said the little prince.

"There is nothing to understand," said the lamplighter. "Orders are orders. Good morning."

And he put out his lamp.

Then he mopped his forehead with a handkerchief decorated with red squares.

"I follow a terrible profession. In the old days it was reasonable. I put the lamp out in the morning, and in the evening I lighted it again. I had the rest of the day for relaxation and the rest of the night for sleep."

"And the orders have been changed since that time?"

"The orders have not been changed," said the lamplighter. "That is the tragedy! From year to year the planet has turned more rapidly and the orders have not been changed!"

"Then what?" asked the little prince.

"Then—the planet now makes a complete turn every minute, and I no longer have a single second for repose. Once every minute I have to light my lamp and put it out!"

"That is very funny! A day lasts only one minute, here where you live!"

"It is not funny at all!" said the lamplighter. "While we have been talking together a month has gone by."

"A month?"

"Yes, a month. Thirty minutes. Thirty days. Good evening."

And he lighted his lamp again.

As the little prince watched him, he felt that he loved this lamplighter who was so faithful to his orders. He remembered the sunsets which he himself had gone to seek, in other days, merely by pulling up his chair; and he wanted to help his friend.

"You know," he said, "I can tell you a way you can rest whenever you want to…"

"I always want to rest," said the lamplighter.

For it is possible for a man to be faithful and lazy at the same time.

The little prince went on with his explanation:

"Your planet is so small that three strides will take you all the way around it. To be always in the sunshine, you need only walk along rather slowly. When you want to rest, you will walk—and the day will last as long as you like."

"That doesn't do me much good," said the lamplighter. "The one thing I love in life is to sleep."

"Then you're unlucky," said the little prince.

"I am unlucky," said the lamplighter. "Good morning."

And he put out his lamp.

"That man," said the little prince to himself, as he continued farther on his journey, "that man would be scorned by all the others: by the king, by the conceited man, by the tippler, by the businessman. Nevertheless he is the only one of them all who does not seem to me ridiculous. Perhaps that is because he is thinking of something else besides himself."

He breathed a sigh of regret, and said to himself, again:

"That man is the only one of them all whom I could have made my friend. But his planet is indeed too small. There is no room on it for two people…"

What the little prince did not dare confess was that he was sorry most of all to leave this planet, because it was blest every day with 1440 sunsets!

15 🪐

The sixth planet was ten times larger than the last one. It was inhabited by an old gentleman who wrote voluminous books.

"Oh, look! Here is an explorer!" he exclaimed to himself when he saw the little prince coming.

The little prince sat down on the table and panted a little. He had already traveled so much and so far!

"Where do you come from?" the old gentleman said to him.

"What is that big book?" said the little prince. "What are you doing?"

"I am a geographer," said the old gentleman.

"What is a geographer?" asked the little prince.

"A geographer is a scholar who knows the location of all the seas, rivers, towns, mountains, and deserts."

"That is very interesting," said the little prince. "Here at last is a man who has a real profession!" And he cast a look around him at the planet of the geographer. It was the most magnificent and stately planet that he had ever seen.

"Your planet is very beautiful," he said. "Has it any oceans?"

"I couldn't tell you," said the geographer.

"Ah!" The little prince was disappointed. "Has it any mountains?"

"I couldn't tell you," said the geographer.

"And towns, and rivers, and deserts?"

"I couldn't tell you that, either."

"But you are a geographer!"

"Exactly," the geographer said. "But I am not an explorer. I haven't a single explorer on my planet. It is not the geographer who goes out to count the towns, the rivers, the mountains, the seas, the oceans, and the deserts. The geographer is much too important to go loafing about. He does not leave his desk. But he receives the explorers in his study. He asks them questions, and he notes down that they recall of their travels. And if the recollections of any one among them seem interesting

to him, the geographer orders an inquiry into that explorer's moral character."

"Why is that?"

"Because an explorer who told lies would bring disaster on the books of the geographer. So would an explorer who drank too much."

"Why is that?" asked the little prince.

"Because intoxicated men see double. Then the geographer would note down two mountains in a place where there was only one."

"I know some one," said the little prince, "who would make a bad explorer."

"That is possible. Then, when the moral character of the explorer is shown to be good, an inquiry is ordered into his discovery."

"One goes to see it?"

"No. That would be too complicated. But one requires the explorer to furnish proofs. For example, if the discovery in question is that of a large mountain, one requires that large stones be brought back from it."

The geographer was suddenly stirred to excitement.

"But you—you come from far away! You are an explorer! You shall describe your planet to me!"

And, having opened his big register, the geographer sharpened his pencil. The recitals of explorers are put down first in pencil. One waits until the explorer has furnished proofs, before putting them down in ink.

"Well?" said the geographer expectantly.

"Oh, where I live," said the little prince, "it is not very interesting. It is all so small. I have three volcanoes. Two volcanoes are active and the other is extinct. But one never knows."

"One never knows," said the geographer.

"I have also a flower."

"We do not record flowers," said the geographer.

"Why is that? The flower is the most beautiful thing on my planet!"

"We do not record them," said the geographer, "because they are ephemeral."

"What does that mean—'ephemeral'?"

"Geographies," said the geographer, "are the books which, of all books, are most concerned with matters of consequence. They never become old-fashioned. It is very rarely that a mountain changes its position. It is very rarely that an ocean empties itself of its waters. We write of eternal things."

"But extinct volcanoes may come to life again," the little prince interrupted. "What does that mean—'ephemeral'?"

"Whether volcanoes are extinct or alive, it comes to the same thing for us," said the geographer. "The thing that matters to us is the mountain. It does not change."

"But what does that mean—'ephemeral'?" repeated the little prince, who never in his life had let go of a question, once he had asked it.

"It means, 'which is in danger of speedy disappearance.'"

"Is my flower in danger of speedy disappearance?"

"Certainly it is."

"My flower is ephemeral," the little prince said to himself, "and she has only four thorns to defend herself against the world. And I have left her on my planet, all alone!"

That was his first moment of regret. But he took courage once more.

"What place would you advise me to visit now?" he asked.

"The planet Earth," replied the geographer. "It has a good reputation."

And the little prince went away, thinking of his flower.

16 🪐

So then the seventh planet was the Earth.

The Earth is not just an ordinary planet! One can count, there, 111 kings (not forgetting, to be sure, the Negro kings among them), 7000 geographers, 900,000 businessmen, 7,500,000 tipplers, 311,000,000 conceited men—that is to say, about 2,000,000,000 grown-ups.

To give you an idea of the size of the Earth, I will tell you that before the invention of electricity it was necessary to maintain, over the whole of the six continents, a veritable army of 462,511 lamplighters for the street lamps.

Seen from a slight distance, that would make a splendid spectacle. The movements of this army would be regulated like those of the ballet in the opera. First would come the turn of the lamplighters of New Zealand and Australia. Having set their lamps alight, these would go off to sleep. Next, the lamplighters of China and Siberia would enter for their steps in the dance, and then they too would be waved back into the wings. After that would come the turn of the lamplighters of Russia and the Indies; then those of Africa and Europe; then those of South America; then those of North America. And never would they make a mistake in the order of their entry upon the stage. It would be magnificent.

Only the man who was in charge of the single lamp at the North Pole, and his colleague who was responsible for the single lamp at the South Pole—only these two would live free from toil and care: they would be busy twice a year.

17 🪐

🎧 17

When one wishes to play the wit, he sometimes wanders a little from the truth. I have not been altogether honest in what I have told you about the lamplighters. And I realize that I run the risk of giving a false idea of our planet to those who do not know it. Men occupy a very small place upon the Earth. If the two billion inhabitants who people its surface were all to stand upright and somewhat crowded together, as they do for some big public assembly, they could easily be put into one public square twenty miles long and twenty miles wide. All humanity could be piled up on a small Pacific islet.

The grown-ups, to be sure, will not believe you when you tell them that. They imagine that they fill a great deal of space. They fancy themselves as important as the baobabs. You should advise them, then, to make their own calculations. They adore figures, and that will please them. But do not waste your time on this extra task. It is unnecessary. You have, I know, confidence in me.

When the little prince arrived on the Earth, he was very much surprised not to see any people. He was beginning to be afraid he had come to the wrong planet, when a coil of gold, the color of the moonlight, flashed across the sand.

"Good evening," said the little prince courteously.

"Good evening," said the snake.

"What planet is this on which I have come down?" asked the little prince.

"This is the Earth; this is Africa," the snake answered.

"Ah! Then there are no people on the Earth?"

"This is the desert. There are no people in the desert. The Earth is large," said the snake.

The little prince sat down on a stone, and raised his eyes toward the sky.

"I wonder," he said, "whether the stars are set alight in heaven so that one day each one of us may find his own again… Look at my planet. It is right there above us. But how far away it is!"

"It is beautiful," the snake said. "What has brought you here?"

You are a funny animal...
You are no thicker than a finger.

"I have been having some trouble with a flower," said the little prince.

"Ah!" said the snake.

And they were both silent.

"Where are the men?" the little prince at last took up the conversation again. "It is a little lonely in the desert…"

"It is a little lonely among men," the snake said.

The little prince gazed at him for a long time.

"You are a funny animal," he said at last. "You are no thicker than a finger…"

"But I am more powerful than the finger of a king," said the snake.

The little prince smiled.

"You are not very powerful. You haven't even any feet. You cannot even travel…"

"I can carry you farther than any ship could take you," said the snake.

He twined himself around the little prince's ankle, like a golden bracelet.

"Whomever I touch, I send back to the earth from whence he came," the snake spoke again. "But you are innocent and true, and you come from a star…"

The little prince made no reply.

"You move me to pity—you are so weak on this Earth made of granite," the snake said. "I can help you, some day, if you grow too homesick for your own planet. I can—"

"Oh! I understand you very well," said the little prince. "But why do you always speak in riddles?"

"I solve them all," said the snake.

And they were both silent.

18

The little prince crossed the desert and met with only one flower. It was a flower with three petals, a flower of no account at all.

"Good morning," said the little prince.

"Good morning," said the flower.

"Where are the men?" the little prince asked, politely.

The flower had once seen a caravan passing.

"Men?" she echoed. "I think there are six or seven of them in existence. I saw them, several years ago. But one never knows where to find them. The wind blows them away. They have no roots, and that makes their life very difficult."

"Goodbye," said the little prince.

"Goodbye," said the flower.

19 🪐

After that, the little prince climbed a high mountain. The only mountains he had ever known were the three volcanoes, which came up to his knees. And he used the extinct volcano as a foot-stool. "From a mountain as high as this one," he said to himself, "I shall be able to see the whole planet at one glance, and all the people…"

But he saw nothing, save peaks of rock that were sharpened like needles.

"Good morning," he said courteously.

"Good morning—Good morning—Good morning," answered the echo.

"Who are you?" said the little prince.

"Who are you—Who are you—Who are you?" answered the echo.

"Be my friends. I am all alone," he said.

"I am all alone—all alone—all alone," answered the echo.

"What a queer planet!" he thought. "It is altogether dry, and altogether pointed, and altogether harsh and forbidding. And the people have no imagination. They repeat whatever one says to them… On my planet I had a flower; she always was the first to speak…"

What a queer planet. It is altogether dry,
and altogether pointed.

20

B ut it happened that after walking for a long time through sand, and rocks, and snow, the little prince at last came upon a road. And all roads lead to the abodes of men.

"Good morning," he said.

He was standing before a garden, all abloom with roses.

"Good morning," said the roses.

The little prince gazed at them. They all looked like his flower.

"Who are you?" he demanded, thunderstruck.

"We are roses," the roses said.

And he was overcome with sadness. His flower had told him that she was the only one of her kind in all the universe. And here were five thousand of them, all alike, in one single garden!

"She would be very much annoyed," he said to himself, "if she should see that… She would cough most dreadfully, and she would pretend that she was dying,

to avoid being laughed at. And I should be obliged to pretend that I was nursing her back to life—for if I did not do that, to humble myself also, she would really allow herself to die…"

Then he went on with his reflections: "I thought that I was rich, with a flower that was unique in all the world; and all I had was a common rose. A common rose, and three volcanoes that come up to my knees—and one of them perhaps extinct forever… That doesn't make me a very great prince…"

And he lay down in the grass and cried.

And he lay down in the grass and cried.

21 🪐

🎧 21

It was then that the fox appeared.

"Good morning," said the fox.

"Good morning," the little prince responded politely, although when he turned around he saw nothing.

"I am right here," the voice said, "under the apple tree."

"Who are you?" asked the little prince, and added, "You are very pretty to look at."

"I am a fox," the fox said.

"Come and play with me," proposed the little prince. "I am so unhappy."

"I cannot play with you," the fox said. "I am not tamed."

"Ah! Please excuse me," said the little prince.

But, after some thought, he added:

"What does that mean—'tame'?"

"You do not live here," said the fox. "What is it that you are looking for?"

"I am looking for men," said the little prince. "What does that mean—'tame'?"

"Men," said the fox. "They have guns, and they hunt. It is very disturbing. They also raise chickens. These are their only interests. Are you looking for chickens?"

"No," said the little prince. "I am looking for friends. What does that mean—'tame'?"

"It is an act too often neglected," said the fox. "It means to establish ties."

"'To establish ties'?"

"Just that," said the fox. "To me, you are still nothing more than a little boy who is just like a hundred thousand other little boys. And I have no need of you. And you, on your part, have no need of me. To you, I am nothing more than a fox like a hundred thousand other foxes. But if you tame me, then we shall need each other. To me, you will be unique in all the world. To you, I shall be unique in all the world…"

"I am beginning to understand," said the little prince. "There is a flower… I think that she has tamed me…"

"It is possible," said the fox. "On the Earth one sees all sorts of things."

"Oh, but this is not on the Earth!" said the little prince.

The fox seemed perplexed, and very curious.

"On another planet?"

"Yes."

"Are there hunters on that planet?"

"No."

"Ah, that is interesting! Are there chickens?"

"No."

"Nothing is perfect," sighed the fox.

But he came back to his idea.

"My life is very monotonous," he said. "I hunt chickens; men hunt me. All the chickens are just alike, and all the men are just alike. And, in consequence, I am a little bored. But if you tame me, it will be as if the sun came to shine on my life. I shall know the sound of a step that will be different from all the others. Other steps send me hurrying back underneath the ground. Yours will call me, like music, out of my burrow. And then look: you see the grain-fields down yonder? I do not eat bread. Wheat is of no use to me. The wheat fields have nothing to say to me. And that is sad. But you have hair that is the color of gold. Think how wonderful that will be when you have tamed me! The grain, which is also golden, will bring me back the thought of you. And I shall love to listen to the wind in the wheat…"

The fox gazed at the little prince, for a long time.

"Please—tame me!" he said.

"I want to, very much," the little prince replied. "But

I have not much time. I have friends to discover, and a great many things to understand."

"One only understands the things that one tames," said the fox. "Men have no more time to understand anything. They buy things all ready made at the shops. But there is no shop anywhere where one can buy friendship, and so men have no friends any more. If you want a friend, tame me…"

"What must I do, to tame you?" asked the little prince.

"You must be very patient," replied the fox. "First you will sit down at a little distance from me—like that—in the grass. I shall look at you out of the corner of my eye, and you will say nothing. Words are the source of misunderstandings. But you will sit a little closer to me, every day…"

The next day the little prince came back.

"It would have been better to come back at the same hour," said the fox. "If, for example, you come at four o'clock in the afternoon, then at three o'clock I shall begin to be happy. I shall feel happier and happier as the hour advances. At four o'clock, I shall already be worrying and jumping about. I shall show you how

If you come at four o'clock in the afternoon,
then by three o'clock I shall begin to be happy.

happy I am! But if you come at just any time, I shall never know at what hour my heart is to be ready to greet you… One must observe the proper rites…"

"What is a rite?" asked the little prince.

"Those also are actions too often neglected," said the fox. "They are what make one day different from other days, one hour from other hours. There is a rite, for example, among my hunters. Every Thursday they dance with the village girls. So Thursday is a wonderful day for me! I can take a walk as far as the vineyards. But if the hunters danced at just any time, every day would be like every other day, and I should never have any vacation at all."

So the little prince tamed the fox. And when the hour of his departure drew near—

"Ah," said the fox, "I shall cry."

"It is your own fault," said the little prince. "I never wished you any sort of harm; but you wanted me to tame you…"

"Yes, that is so," said the fox.

"But now you are going to cry!" said the little prince.

"Yes, that is so," said the fox.

"Then it has done you no good at all!"

"It has done me good," said the fox, "because of the color of the wheat fields." And then he added:

"Go and look again at the roses. You will understand now that yours is unique in all the world. Then come back to say goodbye to me, and I will make you a present of a secret."

The little prince went away, to look again at the roses.

"You are not at all like my rose," he said. "As yet you are nothing. No one has tamed you, and you have tamed no one. You are like my fox when I first knew him. He was only a fox like a hundred thousand other foxes. But I have made him my friend, and now he is unique in all the world."

And the roses were very much embarrassed.

"You are beautiful, but you are empty," he went on. "One could not die for you. To be sure, an ordinary passerby would think that my rose looked just like you—the rose that belongs to me. But in herself alone she is more important than all the hundreds of you other roses: because it is she that I have watered; because it is she that I have put under the glass globe; because it is she that I have sheltered behind the screen; because it is for her that I have killed the caterpillars (except the two

or three that we saved to become butterflies); because it is she that I have listened to, when she grumbled, or boasted, or even sometimes when she said nothing. Because she is my rose."

And he went back to meet the fox.

"Goodbye," he said.

"Goodbye," said the fox. "And now here is my secret, a very simple secret: It is only with the heart that one can see rightly; what is essential is invisible to the eye."

"What is essential is invisible to the eye," the little prince repeated, so that he would be sure to remember.

"It is the time you have devoted to your rose that makes your rose so important."

"It is the time I have devoted to my rose—" said the little prince, so that he would be sure to remember.

"Men have forgotten this truth," said the fox. "But you must not forget it. You become responsible, forever, for what you have tamed. You are responsible for your rose…"

"I am responsible for my rose," the little prince repeated, so that he would be sure to remember.

22

🎧 22

"Good morning," said the little prince.

"Good morning," said the railway switchman.

"What do you do here?" the little prince asked.

"I sort out travelers, in bundles of a thousand," said the switchman. "I send off the trains that carry them: now to the right, now to the left."

And a brilliantly lighted express train shook the switchman's cabin as it rushed by with a roar like thunder.

"They are in a great hurry," said the little prince. "What are they looking for?"

"Not even the locomotive engineer knows that," said the switchman.

And a second brilliantly lighted express thundered by, in the opposite direction.

"Are they coming back already?" demanded the little prince.

"These are not the same ones," said the switchman. "It is an exchange."

"Were they not satisfied where they were?" asked the little prince.

"No one is ever satisfied where he is," said the switch-man.

And they heard the roaring thunder of a third brilliantly lighted express.

"Are they pursuing the first travelers?" demanded the little prince.

"They are pursuing nothing at all," said the switch-man. "They are asleep in there, or if they are not asleep they are yawning. Only the children are flattening their noses against the window-panes."

"Only the children know what they are looking for," said the little prince. "They devote their time to a rag doll and it becomes very important to them; and if anybody takes it away from them, they cry…"

"They are lucky," the switchman said.

23 ⌀

"Good morning," said the little prince.

"Good morning," said the merchant.

This was a merchant who sold pills that had been invented to quench thirst. You need only swallow one pill a week, and you would feel no need of anything to drink.

"Why are you selling those?" asked the little prince.

"Because they save a tremendous amount of time," said the merchant. "Computations have been made by experts. With these pills, you save fifty-three minutes in every week."

"And what do I do with those fifty-three minutes?"

"Anything you like…"

"As for me," said the little prince to himself, "if I had fifty-three minutes to spend as I liked, I should walk at my leisure toward a spring of fresh water."

24

24

It was now the eighth day since I had had my accident in the desert, and I had listened to the story of the merchant as I was drinking the last drop of my water supply.

"Ah," I said to the little prince, "these memories of yours are very charming; but I have not yet succeeded in repairing my plane; I have nothing more to drink; and I, too, should be very happy if I could walk at my leisure toward a spring of fresh water!"

"My friend the fox—" the little prince said to me.

"My dear little man, this is no longer a matter that has anything to do with the fox!"

"Why not?"

"Because I am about to die of thirst…"

He did not follow my reasoning, and he answered me:

"It is a good thing to have had a friend, even if one is about to die. I, for instance, am very glad to have had a fox as a friend…"

"He has no way of guessing the danger," I said to

myself. "He has never been either hungry or thirsty. A little sunshine is all he needs…"

But he looked at me steadily, and replied to my thought:

"I am thirsty, too. Let us look for a well…"

I made a gesture of weariness. It is absurd to look for a well, at random, in the immensity of the desert. But nevertheless we started walking.

When we had trudged along for several hours, in silence, the darkness fell, and the stars began to come out. Thirst had made me a little feverish, and I looked at them as if I were in a dream. The little prince's last words came reeling back into my memory:

"Then you are thirsty, too?" I demanded.

But he did not reply to my question. He merely said to me:

"Water may also be good for the heart…"

I did not understand this answer, but I said nothing. I knew very well that it was impossible to cross-examine him.

He was tired. He sat down. I sat down beside him. And, after a little silence, he spoke again:

"The stars are beautiful, because of a flower that

cannot be seen."

I replied, "Yes, that is so." And, without saying anything more, I looked across the ridges of sand that were stretched out before us in the moonlight.

"The desert is beautiful," the little prince added.

And that was true. I have always loved the desert. One sits down on a desert sand dune, sees nothing, hears nothing. Yet through the silence something throbs, and gleams...

"What makes the desert beautiful," said the little prince, "is that somewhere it hides a well..."

I was astonished by a sudden understanding of that mysterious radiation of the sands. When I was a little boy I lived in an old house, and legend told us that a treasure was buried there. To be sure, no one had ever known how to find it; perhaps no one had ever even looked for it. But it cast an enchantment over that house. My home was hiding a secret in the depths of its heart...

"Yes," I said to the little prince. "The house, the stars, the desert—what gives them their beauty is something that is invisible!"

"I am glad," he said, "that you agree with my fox."

As the little prince dropped off to sleep, I took him

in my arms and set out walking once more. I felt deeply moved, and stirred. It seemed to me that I was carrying a very fragile treasure. It seemed to me, even, that there was nothing more fragile on all the Earth. In the moonlight I looked at his pale forehead, his closed eyes, his locks of hair that trembled in the wind, and I said to myself: "What I see here is nothing but a shell. What is most important is invisible…"

As his lips opened slightly with the suspicion of a half-smile, I said to myself, again: "What moves me so deeply, about this little prince who is sleeping here, is his loyalty to a flower—the image of a rose that shines through his whole being like the flame of a lamp, even when he is asleep…" And I felt him to be more fragile still. I felt the need of protecting him, as if he himself were a flame that might be extinguished by a little puff of wind…

And, as I walked on so, I found the well, at daybreak.

25 🪐

🎧 25

"Men," said the little prince, "set out on their way in express trains, but they do not know what they are looking for. Then they rush about, and get excited, and turn round and round…"

And he added:

"It is not worth the trouble…"

The well that we had come to was not like the wells of the Sahara. The wells of the Sahara are mere holes dug in the sand. This one was like a well in a village. But there was no village here, and I thought I must be dreaming…

"It is strange," I said to the little prince. "Everything is ready for use: the pulley, the bucket, the rope…"

He laughed, touched the rope, and set the pulley to working. And the pulley moaned, like an old weathervane which the wind has long since forgotten.

"Do you hear?" said the little prince. "We have wakened the well, and it is singing…"

I did not want him to tire himself with the rope.

"Leave it to me," I said. "It is too heavy for you."

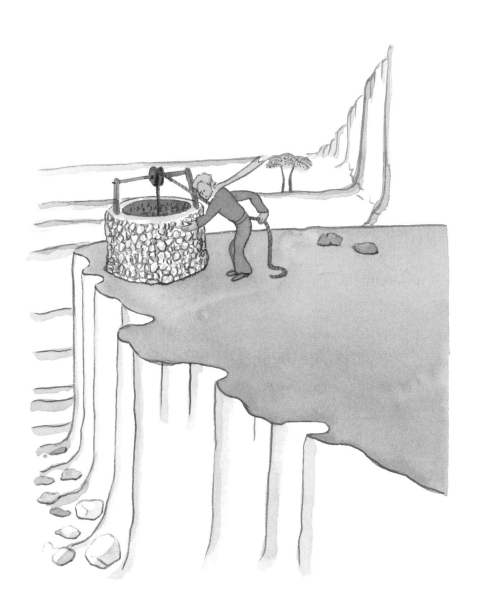

He laughed, touched the rope,
and set the pulley to working.

I hoisted the bucket slowly to the edge of the well and set it there—happy, tired as I was, over my achievement. The song of the pulley was still in my ears, and I could see the sunlight shimmer in the still trembling water.

"I am thirsty for this water," said the little prince. "Give me some of it to drink…"

And I understood what he had been looking for.

I raised the bucket to his lips. He drank, his eyes closed. It was as sweet as some special festival treat. This water was indeed a different thing from ordinary nourishment. Its sweetness was born of the walk under the stars, the song of the pulley, the effort of my arms. It was good for the heart, like a present. When I was a little boy, the lights of the Christmas tree, the music of the Midnight Mass, the tenderness of smiling faces, used to make up, so, the radiance of the gifts I received.

"The men where you live," said the little prince, "raise five thousand roses in the same garden—and they do not find in it what they are looking for."

"They do not find it," I replied.

"And yet what they are looking for could be found in one single rose, or in a little water."

"Yes, that is true," I said.

And the little prince added:

"But the eyes are blind. One must look with the heart…"

I had drunk the water. I breathed easily. At sunrise the sand is the color of honey. And that honey color was making me happy, too. What brought me, then, this sense of grief?

"You must keep your promise," said the little prince, softly, as he sat down beside me once more.

"What promise?"

"You know—a muzzle for my sheep… I am responsible for this flower…"

I took my rough drafts of drawings out of my pocket. The little prince looked them over, and laughed as he said:

"Your baobabs—they look a little like cabbages."

"Oh!"

I had been so proud of my baobabs!

"Your fox—his ears look a little like horns; and they are too long."

And he laughed again.

"You are not fair, little prince," I said. "I don't know how to draw anything except boa constrictors from the

outside and boa constrictors from the inside."

"Oh, that will be all right," he said, "children understand."

So then I made a pencil sketch of a muzzle. And as I gave it to him my heart was torn.

"You have plans that I do not know about," I said.

But he did not answer me. He said to me, instead:

"You know—my descent of the earth… Tomorrow will be its anniversary."

Then, after a silence, he went on:

"I came down very near here."

And he flushed.

And once again, without understanding why, I had a queer sense of sorrow. One question, however, occurred to me:

"Then it was not by chance that on the morning when I first met you—week ago—you were strolling along like that, all alone, a thousand miles from any inhabited region? You were on your way back to the place where you landed?"

The little prince flushed again.

And I added, with some hesitancy:

"Perhaps it was because of the anniversary?"

The little prince flushed once more. He never answered questions—but when one flushes does that not mean "Yes"?

"Ah," I said to him, "I am a little frightened—"

But he interrupted me.

"Now you must work. You must return to your engine. I will be waiting for you here. Come back tomorrow evening…"

But I was not reassured. I remembered the fox. One runs the risk of weeping a little, if one lets himself be tamed…

26

Beside the well there was the ruin of an old stone wall. When I came back from my work, the next evening, I saw from some distance away my little prince sitting on top of this wall, with his feet dangling. And I heard him say:

"Then you don't remember. This is not the exact spot."

Another voice must have answered him, for he replied to it:

"Yes, yes! It is the right day, but this is not the place."

I continued my walk toward the wall. At no time did I see or hear anyone. The little prince, however, replied once again:

"—Exactly. You will see where my track begins, in the sand. You have nothing to do but wait for me there. I shall be there tonight."

I was only twenty meters from the wall, and I still saw nothing.

After a silence the little prince spoke again:

"You have good poison? You are sure that it will not make me suffer too long?"

I stopped in my tracks, my heart torn asunder; but still I did not understand.

"Now go away," said the little prince. "I want to get down from the wall."

I dropped my eyes, then, to the foot of the wall—and I leaped into the air. There before me, facing the little prince, was one of those yellow snakes that take just thirty seconds to bring your life to an end. Even as I was digging into my pocket to get out my revolver I made a running step back. But, at the noise I made, the snake let himself flow easily across the sand like the dying spray of a fountain, and, in no apparent hurry, disappeared, with a light metallic sound, among the stones.

I reached the wall just in time to catch my little man in my arms; his face was white as snow.

"What does this mean?" I demanded. "Why are you talking with snakes?"

I had loosened the golden muffler that he always wore. I had moistened his temples, and had given him some water to drink. And now I did not dare ask him any more questions. He looked at me very gravely, and

Now go away.
I want to get down from the wall.

put his arms around my neck. I felt his heart beating like the heart of a dying bird, shot with someone's rifle…

"I am glad that you have found what was the matter with your engine," he said. "Now you can go back home—"

"How do you know about that?"

I was just coming to tell him that my work had been successful, beyond anything that I had dared to hope.

He made no answer to my question, but he added:

"I, too, am going back home today…"

Then, sadly—

"It is much farther… It is much more difficult…"

I realized clearly that something extraordinary was happening. I was holding him close in my arms as if he were a little child; and yet it seemed to me that he was rushing headlong toward an abyss from which I could do nothing to restrain him…

His look was very serious, like someone lost far away.

"I have your sheep. And I have the sheep's box. And I have the muzzle…"

And he gave me a sad smile.

I waited a long time. I could see that he was reviving little by little.

"Dear little man," I said to him, "you are afraid…"

He was afraid, there was no doubt about that. But he laughed lightly.

"I shall be much more afraid this evening…"

Once again I felt myself frozen by the sense of something irreparable. And I knew that I could not bear the thought of never hearing that laughter any more. For me, it was like a spring of fresh water in the desert.

"Little man," I said, "I want to hear you laugh again."

But he said to me:

"Tonight, it will be a year… My star, then, can be found right above the place where I came to the Earth, a year ago…"

"Little man," I said, "tell me that it is only a bad dream—this affair of the snake, and the meeting-place, and the star…"

But he did not answer my plea. He said to me, instead:

"The thing that is important is the thing that is not seen…"

"Yes, I know…"

"It is just as it is with the flower. If you love a flower that lives on a star, it is sweet to look at the sky at night.

All the stars are abloom with flowers…"

"Yes, I know…"

"It is just as it is with the water. Because of the pulley, and the rope, what you gave me to drink was like music. You remember—how good it was."

"Yes, I know…"

"And at night you will look up at the stars. Where I live everything is so small that I cannot show you where my star is to be found. It is better, like that. My star will be just one of the stars, for you. And so you will love to watch all the stars in the heavens… They will all be your friends. And, besides, I am going to make you a present…"

He laughed again.

"Ah, little prince, dear little prince! I love to hear that laughter!"

"That is my present. Just that. It will be as it was when we drank the water…"

"What are you trying to say?"

"All men have the stars," he answered, "but they are not the same things for different people. For some, who are travelers, the stars are guides. For others they are no more than little lights in the sky. For others, who are

scholars, they are problems. For my businessman they were wealth. But all these stars are silent. You—you alone—will have the stars as no one else has them—"

"What are you trying to say?"

"In one of the stars I shall be living. In one of them I shall be laughing. And so it will be as if all the stars were laughing, when you look at the sky at night… You—only you—will have stars that can laugh!"

And he laughed again.

"And when your sorrow is comforted (time soothes all sorrows) you will be content that you have known me. You will always be my friend. You will want to laugh with me. And you will sometimes open your window, so, for that pleasure… And your friends will be properly astonished to see you laughing as you look up at the sky! Then you will say to them, 'Yes, the stars always make me laugh!' And they will think you are crazy. It will be a very shabby trick that I shall have played on you…"

And he laughed again.

"It will be as if, in place of the stars, I had given you a great number of little bells that knew how to laugh…"

And he laughed again. Then he quickly became serious:

"Tonight—you know… Do not come."

"I shall not leave you," I said.

"I shall look as if I were suffering. I shall look a little as if I were dying. It is like that. Do not come to see that. It is not worth the trouble…"

"I shall not leave you."

But he was worried.

"I tell you—it is also because of the snake. He must not bite you. Snakes—they are malicious creatures. This one might bite you just for fun…"

"I shall not leave you."

But a thought came to reassure him:

"It is true that they have no more poison for a second bite."

That night I did not see him set out on his way. He got away from me without making a sound. When I succeeded in catching up with him he was walking along with a quick and resolute step. He said to me merely:

"Ah! You are there…"

And he took me by the hand. But he was still worrying.

"It was wrong of you to come. You will suffer. I shall look as if I were dead; and that will not be true…"

I said nothing.

"You understand… It is too far. I cannot carry this body with me. It is too heavy."

I said nothing.

"But it will be like an old abandoned shell. There is nothing sad about old shells…"

I said nothing.

He was a little discouraged. But he made one more effort:

"You know, it will be very nice. I, too, shall look at the stars. All the stars will be wells with a rusty pulley. All the stars will pour out fresh water for me to drink…"

I said nothing.

"That will be so amusing! You will have five hundred million little bells, and I shall have five hundred million springs of fresh water…"

And he too said nothing more, because he was crying…

"Here it is. Let me go on by myself."

And he sat down, because he was afraid. Then he said, again:

"You know—my flower… I am responsible for her. And she is so weak! She is so naïve! She has four thorns, of no use at all, to protect herself against all the world…"

I too sat down, because I was not able to stand up any longer.

"There now—that is all…"

He still hesitated a little; then he got up. He took one step. I could not move.

There was nothing there but a flash of yellow close to his ankle. He remained motionless for an instant. He did not cry out. He fell as gently as a tree falls. There was not even any sound, because of the sand.

And he sat down,
because he was afraid.

27 🪐

🎧 27

And now six years have already gone by... I have never yet told this story. The companions who met me on my return were well content to see me alive. I was sad, but I told them: "I am tired."

Now my sorrow is comforted a little. That is to say—not entirely. But I know that he did go back to his planet, because I did not find his body at daybreak. It was not such a heavy body... And at night I love to listen to the stars. It is like five hundred million little bells...

But there is one extraordinary thing... When I drew the muzzle for the little prince, I forgot to add the leather strap to it. He will never have been able to fasten it on his sheep. So now I keep wondering: what is happening on his planet? Perhaps the sheep has eaten the flower...

At one time I say to myself: "Surely not! The little prince shuts his flower under her glass globe every night, and he watches over his sheep very carefully..." Then I am happy. And there is sweetness in the laughter

He fell as gently as a tree falls.
There was not even any sound.

of all the stars.

But at another time I say to myself: "At some moment or other one is absent-minded, and that is enough! On some one evening he forgot the glass globe, or the sheep got out, without making any noise, in the night…" And then the little bells are changed to tears…

Here, then, is a great mystery. For you who also love the little prince, and for me, nothing in the universe can be the same if some where, we do not know where, a sheep that we never saw has—yes or no?—eaten a rose…

Look up at the sky. Ask yourselves: Is it yes or no? Has the sheep eaten the flower? And you will see how everything changes…

And no grown-up will ever understand that this is a matter of so much importance!

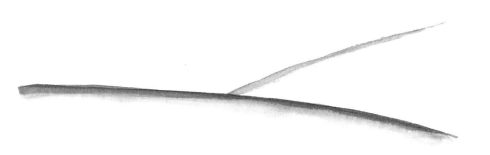

This is, to me, the loveliest and saddest landscape in the world. It is the same as that on the preceding page, but I have drawn it again to impress it on your memory. It is here that the little prince appeared on Earth, and disappeared.

Look at it carefully so that you will be sure to recognize it in case you travel some day to the African desert. And, if you should, come upon this spot, please do not hurry on. Wait for a time, exactly under the star. Then, if a little man appears who laughs, who has golden hair and who refuses to answer questions, you will know who he is. If this should happen, please comfort me. Send me word that he has come back.

Part Two

小王子

　　我六歲那年，看過一本故事書，書名叫《大自然的真相》，內容是描述有關原始森林的生態，裡面有一幅非常壯觀的圖畫。那是一條大蟒蛇，正在絞殺吞食獵物的情景，現在我把它畫出來。

　　書上說：「大蟒蛇靠緊縮身體來勒死獵物，然後嚼也不嚼地吞下整隻獵物。吞下後，牠們便再也無法動彈，得用上整整六個月的時間，一面睡覺、一面消化獵物。」

　　於是，我將這段驚險的叢林奇遇，仔仔細細地想了一遍，然後用彩色鉛筆把它畫出來。第一次就畫得很成

功，我把它編為《第一號繪畫作品》，就像這個樣子：

　　我把這個傑作拿給大人們看，並問他們害不害怕。

　　沒想到他們卻回答：「害怕？一頂帽子有什麼好怕的呢？」

　　我畫的並不是一頂帽子，而是一條正在消化一隻大象的大蟒蛇。但是，既然大人看不懂，我只好再另外畫一張：我把大蟒蛇內部的樣子畫出來，好讓大人可以看清楚。他們習慣每件事情都被解釋得清清楚楚。這是我的《第二號繪畫作品》：

這一次，大人終於有反應了。他們說，不管是不是可以看得到裡面，以後不要再畫大蟒蛇了，應該專心研讀地理、歷史、算術和文法才對。為此，就在我六歲時，放棄了以後可能成為一位偉大畫家的機會。第一號和第二號作品的失敗，讓我失去鬥志。大人們自己什麼事都不懂，總是要讓身為小孩的我們為他們解釋，實在是很累人。

　　因此，我選擇了另一種專長——開飛機。我幾乎飛遍世界每個角落；地理學的知識也確實幫了我很大的忙。只要瞄一眼，我就可以分辨出是身在中國大陸，或美國亞利桑那州的上空。當你在夜間迷航時，這樣的知識是很有用的。

　　這輩子，我接觸過不少關切大事的人，也曾在形形色色的成人圈中生活過。我曾就近仔細地觀察他們，結果並沒有改變多少我對他們的看法。

　　有時，遇到看起來比較有見識的，我會試著拿出我的《第一號繪畫作品》（我一直保存著）觀察他的反應，看他是否真的看懂了。但是，不管是男人或女人，他們總是回答：

　　「這是一頂帽子。」

　　之後，我絕對不會跟那個人談起任何有關大蟒蛇、原始叢林或星星的話題。我會降低自己的水準來遷就他，跟他談一些有關橋牌、高爾夫球、政治以及領帶等等的話題。而他則會非常高興，能遇到一位如此通情達理的人。

2

🎧 29

　　因此，我一直都是一個人過活，沒有什麼真正談得來的朋友。直到六年前，有一次我的飛機引擎發生故障，只好在撒哈拉沙漠中迫降。當時，既沒有機械師，也沒有任何旅客與我同行，我只好試著獨自完成這項艱鉅的修復工作。對我來說，這是攸關生死的大事：我所帶的飲水僅能維持約一個星期左右。

　　第一天晚上，我就睡在遠離人煙千里之遙的沙地上。感覺上，比發生船難乘坐救生艇，在汪洋大海中漂流的水手，還要孤絕。所以，你不難想像，黎明時分，當我被一個細小又古怪的聲音吵醒時的驚愕了。那聲音說：

　　「可否請你——幫我畫一隻綿羊？」

　　「什麼？」

　　「幫我畫一隻綿羊！」

　　我倏地跳起，完全嚇呆了。用力地眨了眨眼，仔細地瞧瞧四周，發現有位異常矮小的小傢伙，正用一種很

稍晚，你可以看到他的肖像畫，
那是事後我為他畫的最好的一幅。

嚴肅的眼光審視著我。稍晚，你可以看到他的肖像畫，那是事後我為他畫的最好的一幅。不過，圖畫看起來當然沒有他本人來得吸引人。

說起來，這也不能怪我。自從我六歲那年，大人們挫敗了我的畫家生涯後，除了畫過看得見和看不見身體內部的大蟒蛇外，往後我未曾再畫過任何東西。

此刻，我睜大雙眼瞪著這個突然出現的影像瞧，驚愕得眼睛都快突出來了。別忘了，我當時正身處在遠離人煙千里之遙的沙漠中。況且，這個小傢伙看起來不像是在沙漠中迷路的樣子，也看不出有任何因疲乏、飢餓及口渴而虛弱不堪，或是恐懼的樣子。他實在一點也不像個在沙漠中走失的小孩——在遠離塵囂千里之遙的沙漠中。當我終於能開口講話的時候，我說：

「可是，你在這裡做什麼呢？」

他以一種非常緩慢的語調，彷彿正在說一件十分重要的大事，回覆道：

「可否請你——幫我畫一隻綿羊……？」

　　當不可思議的事件太過強烈且難以抗拒時，是沒有人敢違抗的。雖然，就我看來這實在很荒謬——在遠離塵囂千里之遙並有死亡之虞的當頭，去畫一隻綿羊——不過，我還是從口袋裡拿出一張紙和鋼筆。可是，直到那時我才想起，過去我只學過地理、歷史、算術和文法等科目，所以只好告訴小傢伙（帶著有點不快的語氣），我不會畫畫。他回答我說：

　　「那沒關係！幫我畫一隻綿羊……。」

　　但是我從來沒有畫過綿羊。於是就幫他畫了一張過去常畫的大蟒蛇，是看不見大蟒蛇身體內部情形的那張。當我聽見小傢伙看到畫的反應時，我著實嚇呆了。

　　「不行，不行，不行！我要的不是一隻在大蟒蛇肚子裡的大象。大蟒蛇太危險，大象又太笨重了。我住的地方，每樣東西都很小，我要的是一隻綿羊，幫我畫一隻綿羊。」

　　既然如此，我就畫了一隻綿羊。

　　他仔細地瞧著，然後說：

　　「不行啦！這隻羊看起來病懨懨的，幫我再畫一張。」

　　於是，我又畫了一張。

我的朋友溫和又寬容地笑著。

「你自己看，」他說：「這不是綿羊，這是一隻公羊，牠的頭上有長角。」

因此，我又重新畫了一張。

但，就像前兩次一樣，這張圖還是未能達到他的標準。

「這隻太老了，我想要一隻可以活很久的羊。」

這時，我的耐性已經快被磨光了，因為我急著要開始拆卸飛機引擎。所以，我胡亂地畫了這張圖，並解釋道：

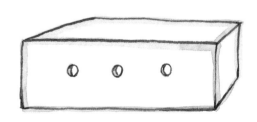

「這是裝著牠的箱子，你要的綿羊就在裡面。」

沒想到，我的小鑑賞家竟面露喜色地說：

「這正是我想要的！你想，牠需要吃很多的草嗎？」

「為什麼這麼問？」

「因為我住的地方，每樣東西都很小……。」

「那裡的草絕對夠牠吃，」我說，「我畫給你的是一隻非常小的綿羊。」

他低頭端詳著圖畫：

「沒那麼小……。你看！牠睡著了……。」

這就是我認識小王子的經過。

3

30

　　我花了不少的時間，才搞清楚他是從哪來的。小王子問了我很多問題，可是卻從未聽進我問他的問題。我是從他的談話當中，一點一滴慢慢拼湊出來的。

　　例如，他第一次看到我的飛機時（飛機對我來說太複雜了，我就不畫了），他問我：

　　「那是什麼東西呀？」

　　「那不是東西。它可以飛，是一架飛機。我的飛機。」

　　我很得意讓他知道我會飛行。

　　他接著巷立即叫道：

　　「什麼？你是從天上掉下來的？」

　　「沒錯！」我謙虛地答道。

　　「噢！真有意思！」

　　小王子很可愛地哈哈大笑，這讓我有點生氣，因為我希望別人能用嚴肅的態度，來看待我的不幸。

　　過了一會，他又說：

　　「這麼說來，你也是從天上來的！你的星球叫什麼
名字？」

　　這時，對於他神祕的出現，百思不得其解的我靈光
一現，一時問道：

　　「你是從別的星球來的嗎？」

　　他沒有回答，只是瞅著我的飛機，輕輕地搖著頭
說：

　　「也對，坐在那個東西上面，你是不可能從很遠的
地方來的……。」

　　之後，有很長一段時間他陷入遐思。接著，他從口
袋裡拿出我畫給他的綿羊，並對著他的寶貝陷入沉思。

　　你不難想像，我的好奇心，已經被那句似真似假的話「別的星球」給挑起。因此，我努力地想找出答案。

「小傢伙，你是從哪裡來的？你所說的『我住的地方』是在哪裡？你要把綿羊帶到哪裡去？」

在一陣靜默的沉思之後，他說道：

「你給我的這個箱子有個好處，在晚上可以當作牠的房子。」

「是啊！如果你當個聽話的孩子，我還會幫你畫一條繩子，這樣，你就可以在白天的時候把牠拴住。另外，還有一根柱子，將牠拴在上頭。」

但是，小王子似乎被我的提議給嚇住了：

「拴住牠！這想法太奇怪了！」

「如果你不拴著牠，」我說，「牠會到處亂跑，並且走失的。」

我的朋友又爆出一陣大笑：

「你認為牠會跑到哪裡去呢？」

「任何地方都有可能，牠會一直往前跑。」

之後小王子很認真地說：

「那不要緊。我住的地方，所有的東西都很小。」

然後，帶著些許的感傷，他又說：

「一直往前跑，沒有人可以跑多遠的……。」

31

　　於是，我又得知了第二個重要的事實：小王子所住的星球，大概比一棟房子大不了多少！

　　不過，我卻一點也不覺得奇怪。因為我很清楚地知道，除了一些大行星，像是地球、木星、火星、金星，曾被命名外，尚有許許多多的小星球，小到即使用望遠鏡也很難看得見。當有某個天文學家發現其中的一顆時，他不會為它命名，而只是給它編個號碼，譬如「第325號小行星」。

　　我有很好的理由相信小王子來自「B-612號小行星」。

　　這顆小行星只有在一九〇九年的時候，曾被一位土耳其的天文學家，用望遠鏡觀測到一次。

　　為了讓他的發現得到認同，這位天文學家曾在國際天文學會中舉證發表過。但是，因為當時他身上穿的是土耳其服裝，所以沒有人肯相信他說的話。

　　大人就是這樣……。

小王子在B-612號行星上

所幸，為了「B-612號小行星」的名聲，有位土耳其的獨裁者，命令所有的人民改穿歐洲的服裝，違者處死。於是，在一九二〇年，這位天文學家穿著高貴、光鮮亮麗的歐洲服裝，把他的發現重新發表過，結果這一次所有的人都相信了。

我會告訴你這些有關小行星的細節，還有它的編號等，那是為了大人們和他們做事習慣的緣故。大人們偏愛數字。當你告訴他們，你交了一位新朋友時，他們從來不會問你任何重要的問題。譬如說，他們從來不問：「他的聲音聽起來怎樣？他最喜歡玩什麼遊戲？他蒐集蝴蝶嗎？」相反的，他們會問：「他多大年紀？他有幾個兄弟？他多重？他父親的收入有多少？」

只有從這些數字當中，大人們才會認為對他有一些瞭解。

假如你對大人們說：「我看到一棟用玫瑰色磚塊砌成的漂亮房子，窗台上擺著天竺葵，屋頂上停著白鴿。」他們對於這棟房子還是不會有任何概念的，你得跟他們說：「我看到一棟價值兩萬美金的房子。」這時，他們便會叫道：「哇！好漂亮的房子啊！」

　　同樣的，你如果對他們說：「小王子存在的證明，就是他很迷人、他笑過，還有他在找一隻綿羊。如果有人想要一隻綿羊，那就是小王子存在的證明。」可是，告訴他們這些又有什麼用呢？他們只會聳聳肩膀，把你當小孩子看待。但是，如果你對他們說：「小王子來自

B-612號小行星。」那麼，他們便會相信你說的話，而且不會再提出問題來打擾你了。

大人們就是這樣。但也不需要為此而跟他們唱反調，小孩子應該時時對大人們賦予極度的寬容。

當然啦，像我們這般深知人生真義的人，數字對我們來說便無關緊要。我本想以童話的方式來寫這個故事，開頭就像這樣：「從前有一位小王子，他住在一個體積比他大不了多少的星球上，他想要一隻綿羊……。」

對於那些瞭解人生真義的人而言，這樣的說法，我的故事反而會顯得更真實些。

因為我不希望別人用漫不經心的態度來讀這本書，所以在我寫下這些回憶的同時，心裡也承受著極大的悲傷。我的朋友帶著他的綿羊，離開我已經有六年了。我會試著描寫他，為的是想確定自己沒有把他給忘了。把朋友給忘了，是一件很可悲的事。並非每個人都曾有過朋友的，如果我把他給忘了，我也許會變得跟大人一樣，除了數字外，不再對任何事情感到興趣……。

也就是為了這個緣故，我重新買了一盒顏料和幾枝鉛筆。到我這個年紀才重拾畫筆，實在不是一件簡單

的事。尤其是自從六歲之後，除了那兩張看得見大蟒蛇內部，和看不見大蟒蛇內部的畫外，我就再也不曾畫過任何東西了。我當然會盡力把肖像畫得栩栩如生，不過能不能成功，我就沒有把握了。有的畫得還不錯，有的則一點也不像本人。就拿小王子的身高來說，我便拿捏不準：有時畫得太高，有時又太矮。還有衣服的顏色，我也不是十分肯定。所以，我只好儘量摸索，時好時壞的，希望大致上還過得去。

　　相信在某些重要的細節上，我還是有所錯失的。
但是這也不能怪我，因為我的朋友從來沒有為我解說過
任何事情。或許，他認為我跟他是同一類的。可是，天
啊！我真的沒有辦法看穿箱子，看到裡面的綿羊。可能
我已經有點像大人們那樣了，不然就是已經老了。

5

　　每天我都會從我們的談話當中，獲知一些有關小王子的星球，以及他離開那個星球和旅途上的事。這些訊息累積得很慢，因為都是從他的回想中，不經意地說出來的。就是在這種情形下，第三天的時候，我聽到了有關猢猻麵包樹可能造成的災難事件。

　　這一次，我還是得感謝那隻綿羊，因為小王子突然問我——他心裡好像有個天大的疑慮：

　　「綿羊吃矮小的灌木，這是真的嗎？」

　　「是真的。」

　　「耶！我太高興了！」

　　我不明白為什麼綿羊吃小灌木，對他來說這麼重要。不過小王子接著又問：

　　「這麼說來，綿羊也吃猢猻麵包樹了？」

　　我向小王子指明，猢猻麵包樹不是小灌木，相反地，是大得像城堡的樹木。就算他帶一群大象回去，也吃不完一棵猢猻麵包樹。

提到一群大象，小王子笑了起來。

他說：「應該把牠們一隻隻疊起來。」

不過，他又滿有智

慧地說：

「在猢猻麵包樹長
得那麼大以前，開始的
時候不也是很小嗎？」

「一點也沒錯，」
我說。「可是，你為什
麼要綿羊去吃小猢猻麵
包樹呢？」

他立刻答道：

「唉！算了，算了！」

好像他說的事情是顯而易見的。於是，我只好在沒有任
何協助的情況下，自己絞盡腦汁思索這個問題。

事實上，就我知道，小王子所住的星球上──就像
所有的星球一樣──長著有益的植物與有害的植物。因
此，好的種子來自有益的植物，不好的種子來自有害的
植物。可是種子是看不見的。它們在黑黝黝的地底下
沉睡著，直到其中的某一粒產生了強烈甦醒的渴望。

那麼，這粒小種子便會開始舒展自己——起初有點羞
怯地——把可愛的小嫩芽無害地向上朝著太陽生長。
如果這是蘿蔔的幼苗或是玫瑰花的嫩芽，便會任由它
隨處生長。但是，如果是有害的植物，一經辨認確定
後，便需盡速將之鏟除。

現在，在小王子家鄉的星球上，有一些可怕的種子──就是猢猻麵包樹的種子。

星球上的土壤全被猢猻麵包樹給佔滿了。如果太晚發現那是一株猢猻麵包樹的嫩芽，那麼，你就永遠也無法將它鏟除了。它會佈滿整顆星球，樹根更會把星球鑽穿。要是這個星球太小，而猢猻麵包樹太多的話，樹根就會把它撐裂成碎塊……。

「這是紀律問題，」後來小王子對我說：「當你早晨漱洗完畢後，也要立即小心翼翼地幫你的星球漱洗一番。你得經常察看，是否已經把所有的猢猻麵包樹幼苗拔除了，猢猻麵包樹與玫瑰花的幼苗長得非常相似，所以，一旦辨別出不是玫瑰花的幼苗，便需立刻把它拔除。這是一件非常乏味的工作，」小王子又補充道：「不過很簡單。」

有一天，他對我說：「你應該畫一幅漂亮的畫，好讓你住的地方的小孩子們，可以清楚地知道這究竟是怎麼一回事。要是有一天他們去旅行，那會對他們很有用處的。」他又說：「有時候，把今天該做的工作延後幾天也不要緊。但，如果是有關猢猻麵包樹的事情，那就會釀成大禍。我知道有一個星球，住著一位懶惰鬼，他

狒狒麵包樹

曾經忽略了三棵小灌木……。」

　　因此，在小王子向我描述的時候，我便畫了一張
那個星球的圖。我不太喜歡以道德家的口吻說話，可
是，猢猻麵包樹的危險性鮮為人知，而迷失在小行星上
的人，卻都有可能遭受危險。所以，這一次我打破緘
默，「孩子們！」我清楚地說道：「要注意猢猻麵包樹
啊！」

　　我的朋友們，就像我自己一樣，已經置身於這樣的
危險邊緣很久了，卻從不自知。也就是為了他們，我才
如此賣力地畫這張圖。以這種方式來傳達這個教訓，我
所花的一切心力就都值得了。

　　或許你會問：「為什麼在這本書裡，其他的圖畫都
不像猢猻麵包樹這般壯觀，和令人印象深刻呢？」

　　其實答案很簡單，因為我已經試過了，但是都沒有
成功。我在畫猢猻麵包樹的時候，是因為受到迫切需求
的激勵，所以才會畫得比平時好。

6

　啊！小王子！一點一滴地，我終於瞭解到你小小生命因何哀傷的祕密……。長久以來，你唯一的消遣，就是觀賞日落時的那份靜謐之樂。我是在第四天的早晨才明白這一點的，因為當時你對我說：

　「我非常喜愛夕陽。來，現在我們來看夕陽吧！」

　「我們得等一下。」我說。

　「等？等什麼？」

　「等太陽下山呀！我們得等到日落的時候。」

　起初你好像非常震驚，隨即卻笑了起來。你說：

　「我還一直以為仍身在自己的家鄉呢！」

　確實如此。大家都知道，當美國正中午的時候，法國正好是日落時分。假如你能在一分鐘之內飛到法國，就可以從中午直接跳到黃昏。可惜法國太遠了。但是，在你小小的星球上，我的小王子，卻只需把你的椅子移動幾步就行了。所以，只要你喜歡，隨時都可以看到一天的結束與黎明的到來……。

　　「有一天，」你對我說：

　　「我總共看了四十四次的夕陽！」

　　過了一會，你又說：

　　「你知道的，人在悲傷的時候，總愛看夕
陽……。」

　　「這麼說來，在你看了四十四次夕陽的那
天，你很悲傷囉？」我問道。

　　但小王子沒有回答。

在第五天的時候——又像往常一樣，藉由那隻綿羊的緣故——我又再次瞭解了小王子生命裡的祕密。突然地，沒有任何跡象可尋，好像這個疑問是他經過長時間的靜思後產生，他說：

「一隻羊——如果牠吃小灌木的話，是否也吃花呢？」

「羊吃任何牠搆得到的東西。」我說。

「即使是有刺的花也吃嗎？」

「沒錯，即使是有刺的花也吃。」

「那麼，這些刺——有什麼用處呢？」

我真的不知道。當時我正忙著要把一枚卡死在引擎內的螺絲釘擰鬆，我實在非常擔憂，因為我漸漸地瞭解到飛機的故障很嚴重。最讓我感到害怕的是，飲用水已經所剩無幾了。

「這些刺——有什麼用處呢？」

一旦提出問題後，小王子從來不會放棄找出答案。而我正與那枚螺絲釘陷入苦戰，於是，未經思索就說：

「那些刺一點用處也沒有。花有刺是因為它惡毒。」

「噢！」

沉默片刻之後，小王子用一種憤恨的口氣對我叫道：

「我不相信！花是很柔弱又天真的，它們儘可能讓自己安心，因為它們相信它們的刺是非常厲害的武器……。」

我沒有回答。此刻我正對著自己說：「如果再轉不動這顆螺絲釘，我就要用鐵鎚把它敲下來。」小王子又打斷我的思緒：

「你真的相信花……。」

「哦，不！」我叫道，「不，不，不！我什麼都不相信。我是未加思索地便回答你的問題，你沒看到我正忙著要緊的事嗎？」

他嚇呆了似地望著我。

「要緊事！」

他看著我，在他眼裡的我手拿鐵鎚，手指被引擎的潤滑油染黑，彎身朝向一個在他看來十分醜陋的東西上……。

「你說話就跟大人一模一樣！」

這話讓我有點慚愧。不過，他卻又毫不客氣地說道：

「你把所有的事情都混在一起……，你把所有的事情都弄擰了……。」

他真的很生氣，把金黃色的鬈髮在微風中一甩。

「我知道有一個星球，上面住著一位滿臉通紅的先生。他從來不曾聞過花香，看過星星。他從來沒有愛過人，在他一生當中，唯一做過的事便是把數字加起來。而且整天像你一樣，老是說著：『我在忙著要緊事！』而這讓他覺得非常驕傲。其實他不是一個人──他是一個蘑菇！」

「一個什麼？」

「一個蘑菇！」

這時小王子氣得臉都白了。

「花長刺已經有幾百萬年了，而羊吃花也有幾百萬年了。所以，試著去瞭解，花為何辛辛苦苦地長些對它們一點用處也沒有的刺，難道說不是很重要的事嗎？羊與花之間的戰爭不重要嗎？難道這不會比一位肥胖紅臉先生的加法來得重要嗎？假如我知道，有一朵在這世上

獨一無二的花，除了在我的星球之外，不在別處生長。可是，某天早晨，有一隻小綿羊很可能在無意中一口把它給吃了——啊！你卻認為這不重要！」

他的臉由白變紅，繼續說著：

「要是一個人愛著一朵花，在千千萬萬的星群裡，唯有它盛開著，只要看著星星，也會讓他覺得快樂。他可以對自己說：『我的花就在那裡的某個地方……。』但是，如果綿羊把花給吃了，剎那間，所有的星星都會變得晦暗。而你卻認為這不重要！」

他已經泣不成聲，說不下去了。

暮色已沉，我丟下手中的工具。此刻，我的鐵鎚、螺絲釘、口渴和死亡，又有什麼要緊呢？在某顆星，某個星球——我的星球，地球上——有位小王子正需要人安慰。我把他摟入懷中，輕輕地搖著，並對他說：

「你鍾愛的花不會有危險，我會幫你的綿羊畫一副口套，在你的花周圍畫一道欄杆。我會……。」

我真的不知道該對他說些什麼。我感到既笨拙又冒失，我不知道如何才能達到再度與他攜手並進的境界。

淚鄉，就是一個如此神祕的國度。

8

很快地，我對這朵花便有了更深的瞭解。在小王子星球上的花都很單純，它們只有一層花瓣，不佔空間也不麻煩人。早晨它們在草叢裡綻放，到了晚上便靜靜地凋落。但是，有一天，不知從哪裡飄來的一粒種子，冒出了新芽，小王子非常密切地觀察這株幼苗，發現它跟星球上其他的幼苗長得不一樣。你看吧，這很有可能是猢猻麵包樹的新品種。

可是過沒多久，這株灌木便停止生長，並且即將開花。首先，小王子看到了一枚碩大的花苞，總覺得會有某種神奇、不可思議的東西從花苞裡蹦出來。但是，這朵花對漂亮的綠萼尚未感到滿意，仍不停地為她的美麗而準備著。她非常仔細地選顏色，慢慢地妝扮自己，一片一片地整理著花瓣。她不希望像田裡的罌粟花一樣，開得縐巴巴、亂糟糟地來到這個世界。她要在她最豔麗照人的時刻出現。啊！是的，她是個風情萬千的尤物！她神祕的妝扮維持了好一段時間。

然後，有一天早晨，就在太陽昇起的時候，她忽然亮相了。

在所有這些辛勤、仔細的工作之後，她卻打著哈欠說道：

「噯！我還沒完全清醒過來呢！真不好意思，我的花瓣還沒梳整好……。」

但是小王子已經禁不住地讚嘆：

「哦！妳好美呀！」

「是嗎？」她溫柔地回答說：「我還是和太陽同時出生的呢……。」

小王子看得出來她不懂得謙虛──不過，她是那麼的動人與教人愛戀！

「我想該吃早餐了，」她緊接著說道：「如果你能夠體貼地想到我的需要……。」

小王子十分尷尬地，趕緊去找了一個裝滿清水的灑水器。於是，他便一直照顧著這朵花。

　　因此，很快地，她也用著她的虛榮心來折磨小王子——如果瞭解真相的話，就會知道這實在有些難以應付。好比說，有一天，在她提到她的四根刺時，她對小王子說：

　　「有著利爪的老虎們來吧！」

　　「在我的星球上沒有老虎，」小王子反駁道：「而且，老虎是不吃雜草的。」

　　「我不是雜草。」那朵花溫柔地回答著。

　　「對不起……。」

「我一點也不怕老虎。」她繼續說道：「但是我怕吹風，我想你沒有幫我準備屏風吧？」

「怕吹風——對一棵植物來說是很不幸的。」小王子評論道，接著自言自語起來：「這朵花真是個非常複雜的生物……。」

「晚上的時候，你要用玻璃罩把我罩住，你住的地方太冷了，我來的地方……。」

但是說到這裡，她就自己打住了。她來到這裡的時候還是一顆種子，不可能知道任何其他世界的事情。為了避免自己天真的謊言被抓到把柄，她困窘地以兩、三聲咳嗽來掩飾，好把所有的過錯都往小王子身上推。

「屏風呢？」

「我正要去找的時候，你又對我說起話來……。」

這時，她又強迫自己多咳幾聲，好讓小王子覺得良心不安。

　　因此，儘管小王子對她的愛與善意討好依舊，但很快地，仍不禁對她有所懷疑。他把她那些無關緊要的話看得太嚴重了，而這樣讓他很不快樂。

　　「我實在不應該聽她的話，」有一天他向我傾訴。「人永遠不要聽花的話，只要單純地欣賞，聞聞她們的花香就好。我那朵花讓我的星球到處花香四溢，但是我卻不知道該如何由她的恩賜中得到快樂。那個有關利爪的故事，原本我應該只是對她充滿關懷與憐惜，但是卻讓我如此不安。」

　　他接著吐露道：

　　「事實是，我不知道該如何去瞭解事情的真相！我應該以行為而非語言來作判斷。她對我展露她的嬌艷，散發她的芳香，我實在不應該逃離她……，我應該看出在她那些可憐的小詭計背後所隱藏的情感。花都是那麼地矛盾！可是，我太年輕了，不知道怎麼去愛她……。」

9

🎧36

　　我想，他是利用一群野生候鳥遷移時逃離的。在臨走的那天早晨，他把他的星球整理得非常妥善。他仔細地清理了他的活火山。他擁有兩座活火山，在早晨用來熱早餐非常方便。同時，他還有一座死火山，不過，正如他所說的：「什麼事都可能發生！」所以，他也很仔細地把死火山清理乾淨。如果清理得很乾淨，火山就不會爆發，只會慢慢地、穩定地燃燒。火山爆發就好像煙囪裡起火一樣。

　　很顯然地，我們實在太渺小了，所以沒辦法清理地球上的火山。這也就是為什麼，火山不斷地為我們帶來麻煩的原因。

　　小王子有些感傷地，也把最後的一些猢猻麵包樹幼苗拔除。他相信自己不會再回來了，可是，在這最後一天的早晨，所有這些熟悉的工作，對他來說似乎顯得特別珍貴。當他幫那朵花澆最後一次水，並準備為她罩上玻璃罩的時候，他發現自己的眼淚幾乎要奪眶而出了。

他仔細地清理他的活火山。

「再見了！」他對那朵花說。

可是她沒有回答。

「再見！」他又說了一次。

那花咳了起來，但不是因為她感冒的緣故。

最後，她對他說：「我以前很傻，請你原諒我，並想辦法讓自己快樂起來……。」

他很驚訝居然沒有任何責備的話，愣愣地站在那裡，雙手拿著玻璃罩停在半空中，對於這種靜謐的甜蜜感到很不習慣。

　　「我當然是愛你的，」花對他說：「你卻一直都不知道，我想這都該怪我。不過這不是重點，重點是——你竟和我一樣的傻。讓自己快樂起來⋯⋯。不要再管那個玻璃罩，我已經不需要了。」

　　「可是，風⋯⋯。」

　　「我的感冒沒有那麼嚴重⋯⋯，夜晚清涼的空氣對我有益。別忘了，我是一朵花。」

　　「可是，動物⋯⋯。」

　　「唉！如果我想跟蝴蝶交朋友的話，總得先忍受兩、三隻毛毛蟲呀！聽說蝴蝶非常的漂亮。況且，除了蝴蝶和毛毛蟲外，還有誰會來看我？你就要遠行了⋯⋯。至於大動物，我一點也不怕牠們——我有利爪。」

　　她很天真地展示了她的四根刺，接著又說：

　　「別這麼依依不捨，既然決定要離開，現在就走吧！」

　　她不想讓小王子看到她哭泣。因為，她是一朵如此驕傲的花⋯⋯。

10

他發現自己身處於第325、326、327、328、329和330號小行星附近，因此，便先開始拜訪這些小行星，以便增長見聞。

第一個小行星上面住著一位國王，他身穿高貴的紫色貂皮大衣，坐在一張簡單卻很莊嚴的寶座上。

「啊！有一位臣民來了。」當國王看到小王子的時候，他叫道。

小王子心想：

「他以前從來沒見過我，怎麼會認得我是他的臣民呢？」

小王子不曉得，這個世界對國王來說是很單純的——除了國王自己以外，所有的人都是他的臣民。

「走近一點，好讓我可以看清楚些。」國王說道。他感到非常驕傲，因為終於有人被他統治了。

小王子四處瞧著，想找個地方坐下來。可是，整個星球都被國王華麗的貂皮長袍給塞滿了，所以他只好筆直站著。站累了，便打起呵欠來。

「在君王面前打呵欠是不合禮法的，」國王說：「我不准你打呵欠。」

「我忍不住啊！我控制不了自己，」小王子十分困窘地答道：「我剛長途跋涉而來，還沒有好好休息……。」

「啊！那麼，」國王說：「我命令你打呵欠。我已經有很多年未曾見到人打呵欠了。打呵欠對我來說，是件很新鮮的事。現在來吧！再打呵欠！這是命令。」

「好可怕……，我打不出呵欠來了……，」小王子喃喃地說著，心裡感到非常惶惑不安。

「嗯！嗯！」國王答道：「那麼——我命令你一會打呵欠，一會……。」

他有點含糊，又有點惱怒地說著。

基本上，國王所堅持的是他的權威要受到尊重，絕對不容許有人違抗。他是一個有獨裁權的君王。可是，因為他心地非常善良，所以下達的命令都很合理。

「要是我命令一位將軍，」他舉例說道：「要是我命令一位將軍把自己變成一隻海鳥，而這位將軍沒有遵從我的命令，那不是這位將軍的錯，應該是我的錯。」

「我可以坐下嗎？」小王子有些膽怯地問道。

「我命令你坐下。」國王回答著，並一面莊嚴地把他的貂皮斗篷收進一褶。

可是小王子覺得很好奇——這個星球那麼小，國王能真的統治些什麼呢？

「陛下，」他對國王說：「請容許我問您一個問題……。」

「我命令你發問。」國王很快地告訴他。

「陛下，您統治些什麼呢？」

「統治一切。」國王威嚴又簡潔地說。

「統治一切？」

國王做了一個手勢，指著他的星球、其他的星球和所有的星星。

「全部都是？」小王子問。

「全部都是。」國王答道。

因為他的統治不僅是獨裁的，還是遍及全宇宙的。

「這些星星會聽從你的命令嗎？」

「當然。」國王說：「它們會馬上遵從，我不允許有人抗命。」

這樣的權力令小王子讚嘆不已。假如他能擁有這麼大的權力，那他在一天之內，就可以欣賞到不只四十四次的夕陽，而是七十二次，或一百次，或甚至二百次，也不必移動他的椅子。這時他想起了那顆被他遺棄的小星球，感到有點悲傷，於是他鼓起勇氣請求國王幫忙：

「我想看夕陽……。請您幫我……命令太陽下山……。」

「如果我命令一位將軍像隻蝴蝶一樣，從一朵花飛到另一朵花，或寫一齣悲劇，或是把自己變成一隻海鳥，要是這位將軍沒有執行所接到的命令，那麼，你說，我們兩個是誰錯了呢？」國王問道：「是將軍，還是我自己？」

「是你不對。」小王子很肯定地說。

「完全正確。我們只能要求別人去做他能夠履行的任務，」國王繼續道：「可被人接受的權威，首先建立在合理的基礎上。如果你命令你的子民去投海，他們一定會起義革命。我有權力要求服從，是因為我的命令很合理。」

「那麼我的夕陽呢？」小王子提醒他：因為他一旦提出問題，就決不會把它給忘了。

「你會看到你要的夕陽，我會下命令的。不過，根據我的統治科學，我得等到有利的時機。」

「什麼時候才是有利的時機呢？」小王子問道。

「嗯！嗯！」國王答著，在說出任何話語之前，他翻閱了一本厚厚的曆書。「嗯！嗯！那大概——大概——是在今天晚上七點四十分左右，你會看到我的命令是如何地被奉行！」

小王子打起呵欠來，有點遺憾看不到夕陽。而且，現在他已經開始覺得無聊了。

「我在這裡已經沒有什麼事情可做了，」他對國王說：「所以我應該啟程了。」

「不要走，」國王說。他非常得意終於有個臣民。「不要走，我任命你當部長！」

「什麼部長？」

「司……司法部長！」

「可是這裡沒有人可以審判呀！」

「這很難說，」國王對他說：「我尚未巡視過所有的領土。我太老了，這裡又太小，沒有地方可以駕馬車，走路又太累人。」

「哦，可是我已經看過了！」小王子說著，同時轉身向這個星球的另一頭再看了一眼。那裡就跟這裡一樣，一個人也沒有……。

「那麼，你就審判你自己，」國王回答。「這是最困難的事情。審判自己要比審判別人困難得多。如果你能正直地審判自己，那麼，你就是一位真正的智者。」

「沒錯，」小王子說：「可是，我在任何地方都可以審判我自己，不需要住在這個星球上。」

「嗯！嗯！」國王說：「我有很好的理由相信，在我星球上的某個地方有一隻很老的老鼠，在晚上可以聽到牠的聲音。你可以審判牠，並不時地判牠死刑。這樣，牠能否活命就全看你的審判，可是你每次判刑後都得赦免牠──我們得留牠活命，因為牠是我們僅有的。」

「我，」小王子答道：「不喜歡判任何人死刑。還有，我想我該走了。」

「不要走。」國王說。

小王子已經準備好要啟程了，但又不想惹這位老國王傷心。

「如果陛下希望命令被立即奉行，」他說：「應該給我下一道合理的命令。譬如說，命令我在一分鐘之內離開，在我看來，現在正是有利的時機……。」

　　國王沒有回答，小王子猶豫了一會，嘆了口氣，之後便要離開。

　　「我任命你當大使。」國王急忙喊道。

　　他擺出一副非常威嚴的模樣。

　　「大人就是這麼奇怪，」小王子一面自言自語，一面開始他的旅程。

11

第二個星球上住著一位自負的人。

「啊！啊！有我的崇拜者來訪了！」當他看到小王子前來時，在遠處就叫道。

因為對這位自負的人來說，所有的人都是他的崇拜者。

「早安，」小王子說：「你戴的帽子好古怪。」

「這是用來答禮的，」自負的人答道。

「當人們向我歡呼時，可以舉起來答禮。

可惜的是，從來沒有人經過這裡。」

「真的嗎？」小王子說，他不瞭解這位自負的人所說的話。

「兩手互拍手掌！」自負的人命令道。

小王子鼓起掌來，自負的人便舉起他的帽子答禮。

「這比拜訪國王要有趣多了。」小王子自語道。於是又拍起手來，自負的人也再次舉帽子答禮。

經過五分鐘的練習之後，小王子開始對這種單調的遊戲感到厭煩。

「要怎麼做你才會把帽子放下來呢？」他問道。

可是自負的人沒有聽到他的話。一個自負的人除了讚美的話，是什麼也聽不見的。

「你真的很崇拜我嗎？」他問小王子。

「你說的『崇拜』——是什麼意思？」

「崇拜的意思就是，你認為我是這個星球上最英俊、衣著最好、最富有，以及最聰明的人。」

「可是，在這個星球上就只有你一個人呀！」

「就算是做好事，你還是要一樣的崇拜我。」

「我崇拜你，」小王子說著，輕輕地聳了聳肩膀。「不過，『有人崇拜』究竟有什麼吸引你的地方，為什麼你如此感興趣？」

於是小王子離開了。

「大人們實在非常奇怪。」當小王子繼續他的旅程時，他自言自語地說著。

12

下一個星球住著一位酒鬼。這次訪問的時間很短暫，但是卻讓小王子陷入極度的悲傷。

「你在那裡做什麼？」他問酒鬼。看他一個人默默地坐在一堆空瓶子和裝滿酒的瓶子前面。

「我正在喝酒。」酒鬼神情陰鬱地答道。

「你為什麼要喝酒？」小王子問。

「為了可以忘掉。」酒鬼回答。

「要忘掉什麼？」小王子問道。他已經為他感到難過了。

「忘掉我的羞恥。」酒鬼低下頭來，坦承道。

「什麼羞恥？」小王子追問道，想幫他的忙。

「喝酒的羞恥！」酒鬼說完這句話後，就沉默不語了。

小王子非常困惑地離開了。

「大人真的非常非常奇怪。」在旅途中，他自言自語地說著。

13

第四個星球屬於一個商人所有。這個人實在太忙了，所以小王子到達的時候，他甚至連頭也沒抬起來。

「早安，」小王子對他說：「你的香煙已經熄滅了。」

「三加二等於五。五加七等於十二。十二加三等於十五。早安。十五加七等於二十二。二十二加六等於二十八。我沒有空再把它點燃。二十六加五等於三十一。噢！總共是五億零一百六十二萬二千七百三十一。」

「五億個什麼呀？」小王子問。

「噯？你還在那裡啊？五億零一百萬……。我不能停……。我要做的事情太多了！我只關心重要的事情，我不會說些毫無意義的話來娛樂自己。二加五等於七……。」

「五億零一百萬個什麼？」小王子重複問道。他這輩子只要一提出問題，就從不會放棄。

商人抬起頭來。

「住在這個星球的五十四年當中，我只被打擾過三次。第一次是在二十二年前，當時不知道從哪裡掉下來一隻頭發暈的鵝，牠發出一種非常嚇人的噪音，而且聲音迴盪著整個星球，害我的加法算錯了四次。第二次在十一年前，是因為風濕病發作。我缺乏運動，也沒有時間閒逛。第三次——嗯，就是現在了！我剛剛是在說五億零一百萬……。」

「一百萬個什麼？」

商人突然瞭解到，如果沒有回答這個問題，他是沒有辦法得到安靜的。

「百萬個小東西，」他說：「那些有時候可以在天空中看到的東西。」

「蒼蠅嗎？」

「喔！不對。小小的會發亮的東西。」

「蜜蜂？」

「不是！小小的金黃色的，會讓懶惰的人胡思亂想的東西。至於我，我只關心重要的事，我的人生沒有時間去胡思亂想。」

「啊！你說的是星星？」

「對，沒錯，就是星星。」

「那你要五億顆星星做什麼呢？」

「五億零一百六十二萬二千七百三十一顆。我只關心重要的事──我算得很精準。」

「你要這些星星做什麼？」

「我要它們做什麼？」

「是啊！」

「不做什麼。我擁有它們。」

「你擁有這些星星？」

「不錯。」

「可是，我已經碰過有個國王，他⋯⋯。」

「國王不是擁有，他們是統治。這是非常不同的事。」

「擁有星星對你有什麼好處呢？」

「可以讓我變得很富有。」

「富有對你有什麼好處呢？」

「這樣我就可以買更多的星星──假如有新的星星被發現的話。」

「這個人，」小王子暗道，「這理由有點像那可憐的酒鬼⋯⋯。」

雖然如此，他還是有許多的問題要問。

「一個人怎麼可能擁有星星呢？」

「不然，它們屬於誰呢？」商人微慍地反問道。

「我不知道。不屬於任何人吧！」

「那麼，它們就是屬於我，因為我是第一個想擁有它們的人。」

「這就夠了嗎？」

「當然。若你發現一顆不屬於任何人的鑽石，那它就屬於你。若你發現一座不屬於任何人的島嶼，它就屬於你。若你比別人先想到一個主意，並取得專利，它就是你的。因此，對我來說，我擁有這些星星，因為沒有人比我更早想到要擁有它們。」

「不錯，這倒是真的，」小王子說：「那你要它們做什麼呢？」

「我管理它們，」商人回答。「我把它們數了又數，這事很困難。不過，我是一個天生對重要的事感興趣的人。」

小王子還是不太滿意。

「如果我擁有一條絲綢的圍巾，」他說，「我可以把它圍在脖子上帶著走。如果我擁有一朵花，我可以把它摘下來帶走。可是，你沒辦法從天上把星星摘下

來⋯⋯。」

「沒錯。但是，我可以把它們存在銀行裡。」

「這到底是什麼意思？」

「就是說，我把星星的數目寫在一張小紙條上，然後在把紙條放在抽屜裡用鑰匙鎖上。」

「就這樣？」

「這樣就夠了，」商人說。

「真有趣，」小王子想道：「這滿有詩意的，可是卻不重要。」

對何謂重要的事情，小王子的看法跟大人很不一樣。

「我自己擁有一朵花，」他繼續和商人說道：「我每天幫她澆水。我有三座火山，我每個星期都會把它們清理乾淨（我也清理那座死火山，因為誰也不知道它何時會爆發）。因為這樣對我的火山和花有些用處，所以才擁有它們。可是你對星星一點用處也沒有⋯⋯。」

商人張大嘴巴，卻無言以對。於是，小王子便離開了。

「大人們實在都太奇怪了。」在繼續他的旅程時，小王子只能如此地自語道。

14 🪐

　　第五個星球非常奇特。它是所有的行星中最小的一個，它的大小只能容下一盞路燈和一位燈夫。小王子想不出任何解釋，在天空的某處，一個沒有人住，甚至連一間房子也沒有的星球上，要一盞路燈和一個燈夫有什麼用處。儘管如此，小王子仍暗自想道：

　　「這個人看起來是很荒謬，然而跟國王、自負的人、商人以及酒鬼們比起來就好多了。至少，他的工作較有意義。當他點燃路燈時，就好像多讓一顆星星或一朵花甦醒過來。當他熄燈時，就好像送這朵花或是星星進入夢鄉。這是一件很美的工作。既然很美，也就真的有用了。」

　　抵達這顆星球的時候，他非常恭敬地向燈夫敬禮。

　　「早安。你剛剛為什麼要熄燈呢？」

　　「這是命令，」燈夫答道。「早安。」

　　「是什麼樣的命令？」

　　「就是規定我要熄燈。晚安。」

　　燈夫又把路燈點燃。

我從事的工作很辛苦。

「可是你剛剛為什麼又把它點燃呢？」

「這是命令。」燈夫回答。

「我不懂。」小王子說。

「不需要懂，」燈夫說：「命令就是命令。早安。」

他又把燈熄了。

接著，他用一條有紅色格子的手帕擦額頭。

「我從事的工作很辛苦。以前比較合理，我早上熄燈，晚上點燈。白天剩餘的時間我可以休息，晚上剩餘的時間我可以睡覺。」

「在那之後，命令改變了嗎？」

「命令沒有改，」燈夫說道。「苦就苦在這裡！這個星球旋轉得一年比一年快，可是命令卻從未更改！」

「後來呢？」小王子問。

「後來——這個星球每分鐘便旋轉一圈，我就再也沒有時間休息了。每隔一分鐘，我就要點燈和熄燈一次。」

「那太好玩了！在你住的這個星球，一天只有一分鐘長！」

「這一點也不好玩！」燈夫說。「在我們一起聊天

的這段時間，已經一個月過去了。」

「一個月？」

「沒錯，一個月。三十分鐘，也就是三十天。晚安。」

他又把燈點亮。

小王子望著他，覺得已經喜歡上了這個如此忠於命令的燈夫。他想起了以前追逐夕陽的日子，只要挪動一下自己的椅子就可以了。他想幫他的朋友。

「你知道嘛，」他說：「我可以告訴你一個方法，什麼時候想休息都可以⋯⋯」

「我一直都想休息。」燈夫說。

一個人同時既忠實又懶惰，是很有可能的事。

小王子繼續解釋道：

「你的星球那麼小，你只要走三步就可以繞一周。所以，你只要慢慢地走，就可以永遠地置身在陽光底下。當你想休息時，只要散步──那麼，你想要白天有多長，就有多長。」

「那對我沒有什麼好處，」燈夫說：「我生平最喜歡的事，就是睡覺。」

「那麼你很不幸，」小王子說。

「我是很不幸，」燈夫說道。「早安。」

他又把燈熄滅。

「這個人，」當他繼續接下來的旅程時，小王子自語道：「這個人一定會被其他所有的人嘲笑：像國王、自負的人、酒鬼和商人。雖然如此，他卻是他們之中，我唯一不會覺得荒謬可笑的人。或許，那是因為他思索的是他自身以外的事情。」

他惋惜地嘆了口氣，又自語道：

「這個人是他們之中，唯一一個我想跟他做朋友的人。可是他的星球實在太小了，容納不下兩個人……。」

其實，小王子不敢承認，離開這個星球讓他最感到遺憾的事，是在這裡每天可以看到一千四百四十次的夕陽！

15 🪐

🎧 42

　　第六個星球比上一個星球大了十倍。上面住著一位撰寫很多大部頭書的老先生。

　　「啊！你看！來了一位探險家！」當他看到小王子到來的時候叫道。

　　小王子坐在桌子上，有些氣喘噓噓地。他已經旅行很久，也很遠了！

　　「你從哪裡來呀？」老先生問他說。

　　「那本厚重的書是什麼？」小王子說。「你在做什麼呢？」

　　「我是個地理學家。」老先生說。

　　「什麼是地理學家？」小王子問。

　　「地理學家就是一位知道所有海洋、河流、城鎮、山脈和沙漠位置的學者。」

　　「那真有意思，」小王子說道：「終於有一位有真正職業的人了。」他把地理學家的星球四處瞧了瞧。它是他所見過，最富麗堂皇的星球。

「你的星球真漂亮，」他說：「這裡有海洋嗎？」

「我不清楚。」地理學家說。

「啊！」小王子很失望。「那，這裡有山嗎？」

「我不清楚。」地理學家說。

「有城鎮、河川和沙漠嗎？」

「這個我也不清楚。」

「可是，你是一個地理學家呀！」

「一點也不錯，」地理學家說。「不過我不是個探險家。在我的星球上，連一個探險家也沒有。地理學家的工作不是出外去計算城鎮、河流、山脈、海、大洋和

沙漠的。地理學家太重要了，不能出去閒逛浪費時間。他不會離開他的書桌，可是他會在書房裡接見探險家們。他會向他們提出問題，並把他們旅途中的見聞記錄下來。如果對其中某個見聞感興趣，地理學家就會下令調查這位探險家的品性。」

「為什麼要這麼做呢？」

「因為探險家如果說謊，會給地理學家的書帶來很大的災禍。還有，一個探險家如果酒喝太多的話也會這樣。」

「為什麼會這樣呢？」小王子問道。

「因為喝醉酒的人，會把一個看成兩個。那麼，地理學家就會在只有一座山的地方，記成兩座山。」

「我認識一個人，」小王子說：「他可能會是個很差勁的探險家。」

「那很有可能。接著，如果證明這個探險家的品性良好，便得下令調查他的發現。」

「派人去看嗎？」

「不是，那太麻煩了。會要求探險家拿出證據。譬如說，如果他發現的是一座高山，那他就得從那裡帶回一些大石頭。」

地理學家突然興奮起來。

「不過你——你從遠方來！你是一位探險家！請把你的星球描述給我聽！」

然後，地理學家便翻開他的大筆記本，並削著鉛筆。他把探險家的敘述先以鉛筆記下，等到探險家提出證據後，便改用墨水寫下。

「好了嗎？」地理學家充滿期待地說。

「啊，我住的地方，」小王子說道：「不是很有趣。它很小。我有三座火山。兩座活火山，另一座是死火山。不過，誰也不能確定它會不會再爆發。」

「是沒有人可以確定。」地理學家說。

「我還有一朵花。」

「我們不記錄花。」地理學家說。

「為什麼呢？這朵花是我的星球上最漂亮的一樣東西！」

「我們不記錄花，」地理學家說：「因為她們的生命是『稍縱即逝』的。」

「『稍縱即逝』——是什麼意思？」

「地理學，」地理學家說道：「所有地理學的書，都只記錄重要的事情。它們永遠不會過時。一座山的位

置是不太可能會改變的，海洋裡的水乾涸的機會也是微乎其微。我們寫的都是永恆的東西。」

「但是，死火山是有可能再復活的，」小王子打岔道。「『稍縱即逝』──是什麼意思？」

「不管是死火山或活火山，對我們來說都一樣。」地理學家說。「對我們來說，重要的是山，它不會改變。」

「但是，『稍縱即逝』──是什麼意思？」小王子重複問道。他是一旦提出問題，便永遠不會放棄的人。

「意思是，『有迅速消失的危險。』」

「我的花也有迅速消失的危險嗎？」

「當然有。」

「我的花是稍縱即逝的。」小王子喃喃自語道：「她只有四根刺可以防衛自己，對抗這個世界。而我卻把她留在我的星球上，一個人孤伶伶的！」

這是他第一次感到懊悔。不過，他又再度鼓起勇氣。

「你會建議我現在到哪裡去探訪呢？」他問道。

「地球，」地理學家答道。「它的名聲不錯。」

於是，小王子離開了，心裡一面想念著他的花。

16 🪐

🎧 43

　　因此，第七個星球便是地球。

　　地球可不是個普通的行星呢！算一算，在那裡有一百一十一位國王（當然，不要忘了，非洲土著的國王也包括在內），七千個地理學家，九十萬個商人，七百五十萬個酒鬼，三億一千一百萬個自負的人——也就是說，大約有二十億個大人。

　　為了讓你對地球的大小有個概念，我來告訴你，在電力還沒有發明以前，整個六大洲裡，需要為路燈而贍養四十六萬二千五百一十一個燈夫。

　　從稍遠一點的距離看去，那景象真是壯觀。這些人的動作就好像歌劇中的芭蕾舞者，極有規律地移動著。首先登場的是紐西蘭和澳洲的燈夫，他們把路燈點亮後，便去休息睡覺。其次，中國和西伯利亞的燈夫登場表演後，也揮揮手退入邊廂。接著，輪到蘇俄和印度的燈夫，然後是非洲和歐洲，再來是南美洲、北美洲。他們登台的順序決不會弄錯，那場面實在太浩大壯觀了。

只有在北極的燈夫僅負責一盞路燈，而他在南極的同事也只負責一盞路燈——唯有這兩個人可以悠閒過活，不必那麼辛勞：他們在一年當中只有忙兩次。

17 🪐

　　當一個人想賣弄才智時，有時難免會稍微偏離真相。在我告訴你有關燈夫的事情時，並不是完全誠實的。我知道我可能給那些不瞭解地球的人，一個錯誤的概念。人在地球上所佔的地方很小。如果把地球上的二十億居民全部聚集靠攏，挺直地站在地球表面上，就像在開市民大會一樣，他們可以很容易地一起站在一個二十英里見方的廣場上。全部的人類可以被堆放在一座太平洋中的小島上。

　　當然，如果你這麼告訴大人，他們是不會相信的。大人們認為他們佔有的地方很大，並自以為和猢猻麵包樹一樣重要。因此，你應該建議他們計算一下，他們那麼崇拜數字，這樣會讓他們很高興的。但是，也別把你的時間浪費在這件額外的工作上，那沒有必要。我知道你應該會信任我才對。

　　當小王子抵達地球時，他非常訝異，竟然連一個人看不見。當看到一圈似月光般，金黃色的纏繞物在沙地上閃過時，他開始擔心自己走錯星球。

「晚安。」小王子彬彬有禮地說道。

「晚安。」蛇說。

「我來到的這個星球，是什麼星球？」小王子問。

「這是地球。這裡是非洲。」蛇回答說。

「啊！那麼說，在地球上沒有人囉？」

「這裡是沙漠，沙漠裡沒有人。地球是很大的。」蛇說。

小王子坐在一顆石頭上，抬眼望著天空。

「我在想，」他說：「不知道天上的星星是否都已點燃，這樣有一天，我們每個人可以再找到屬於他自己的星星……。你看我的星球，它就在我們的頭頂上。不過，離得好遠啊！」

「它很美，」蛇說道：「你為什麼會來這裡呢？」

「我和一朵花鬧彆扭。」小王子說。

「噢！」蛇說。

他們都沉默不語。

「哪裡有人呢？」小王子終於又繼續聊起話來。「在沙漠裡有點寂寞……」

「在人群中也會寂寞。」蛇說道。

你是個很有趣的動物……
你還比不上一根手指粗。

小王子注視著他好一會。

「你是個很有趣的動物，」他最後說道：「你還比不上一根手指粗⋯⋯」

「可是我比一個國王的手指還要厲害。」蛇說。

小王子露出微笑：

「你不可能那麼厲害。你沒有腳，你甚至沒辦法旅行⋯⋯。」

「我可以送你到比任何船可以載你去的更遠的地方。」蛇說。

牠把自己纏繞在小王子的腳踝上，就像一隻黃金手鐲似的。

「任何被我碰到的人，我都會把他送回到他來的大地去，」蛇又說道。「但是，你天真又誠實，而且來自一顆遙遠的星星⋯⋯。」

小王子沒有回答。

「你勾起了我的同情心——在這個由花崗石構成的地球上，你太脆弱了。」蛇說：「如果有一天，你太思念你的星球的話，我可以幫助你。我可以⋯⋯」

「噢！我很瞭解你的意思，」小王子說：「可是，為什麼你說話總像在講謎語似的？」

「我會解開所有的謎題。」蛇說。

然後兩人又沉默不語。

18 🪐

　　小王子越過沙漠，只遇見一朵花。那是一朵只有三片花瓣，沒有任何價值的花。

　　「早安。」小王子說。

　　「早安。」花說。

　　「人都在哪裡呢？」小王子很有禮貌地問道。

　　這朵花曾看見一個商隊經過。

　　「人？」她回應道。「我想他們應該還有六、七個人活著吧。幾年前我曾見過他們。可是，沒有人知道在哪裡可以找到他們——風把他們給吹走了。他們沒有根，這樣他們很難存活。」

　　「再見。」小王子說。

　　「再見。」花說。

19 🪐

🎧46

　　在那之後，小王子爬上一座高山。以前他所認識的山，只有那三座高及他膝蓋的火山。而且，他都把那座死火山當作腳凳。「從這麼高的一座山上，」他自言自語道：「應該可以將整個星球和所有的人一覽無遺……。」

　　但是，除了許多鋒利如針的岩石外，他什麼也看不到。

　　「早安。」他謙恭地說道。

　　「早安──早安──早安。」回音答道。

　　「你是誰？」小王子說。

　　「你是誰──你是誰──你是誰？」回音答道。

　　「請你當我的朋友，我好寂寞。」他說。

　　「我好寂寞──好寂寞──好寂寞。」回音回答。

　　「好古怪的星球！」他想道。「一切都是那麼的乾燥、尖利、殘酷和險惡。人們沒有想像力，只會重複別人對他們說的話……。在我的星球上，我有一朵花；她總是先開口說話……。」

好奇怪的星球，
一切都是那麼的乾燥和尖利。

20 🪐

　　但是，在經過沙漠、岩石和雪地的長途跋涉之後，小王子終於來到一條路上。所有的道路都會通向人們的住所。

　　「早安。」他說。

　　他正站在一個玫瑰花盛開的花園前。

　　「早安。」玫瑰花們說。

　　小王子盯著她們瞧。她們看起來都跟他的花好像。

　　「你們是誰？」他非常驚訝地問道。

　　「我們是玫瑰花。」玫瑰花們說。

　　他悲傷不已。他的花曾告訴他，她是全宇宙中僅有的一朵花。但，光是在這座花園裡，就有五千朵長得和她一模一樣的花！

　　「她一定會很生氣，」他自語道：「如果她看到這些花……，她一定會拼命地咳嗽。而且，為了避免被人取笑，她會假裝快要死掉了。而我也不得不裝出一副要細心照顧到她好的模樣——要是我也不如此低聲下氣的話，她會真的讓自己死去……。」

　　接著他又想道：「我本以為我很富有，因為我有一朵舉世無雙的花；然而其實她不過是一朵普通的玫瑰花罷了。一朵普通的玫瑰花、三座及膝的火山——而且其中的一座可能永遠不再爆發……。這些並不足以讓我成為一位偉大的王子……。」

　　於是，他躺在草地上哭了起來。

於是，他躺在草地上哭了起來。

21 🪐

🎧48

就在這個時候，狐狸出現了。

「早安。」狐狸說。

「早安。」小王子有禮貌地回答著，雖然他轉過身時什麼也沒瞧見。

「我就在這裡，」那聲音說：「在蘋果樹下。」

「你是誰？」小王子問，同時說道：「你長得很漂亮。」

「我是一隻狐狸。」狐狸說。

「過來跟我一起玩，」小王子提議道。「我很不快樂。」

「我不能跟你一起玩，」狐狸說：「我還沒有被馴養。」

「哦！對不起。」小王子說。

但是，想了一會後，他又說道：

「『馴養』──是什麼意思？」

「你一定不是住在這裡的人，」狐狸說。「你在找什麼呢？」

「我在找人，」小王子說。「『馴養』──是什麼意思？」

「找人？」狐狸說：「他們有槍，而且打獵，實在

讓人很不安心。他們也養雞，這是他們唯一的好處。你在找雞嗎？」

「不是，」小王子說。「我在找朋友。『馴養』——是什麼意思？」

「那是一種常常被忽略的行為，」狐狸說。「它的意思是建立關係。」

「『建立關係』？」

「不錯，」狐狸說道：「對我來說，你不過是個小男孩，就跟其他成千上萬的小男孩沒有什麼兩樣。我不需要你，而你也不需要我。對你來說，我不過是隻狐狸，跟其他成千上萬的狐狸沒有什麼不同。但是，如果你馴養我，那麼，我們就會彼此需要了。對我來說，你就是這個世上獨一無二的。對你來說，我也是全世界獨一無二的……。」

「我開始有點瞭解了，」小王子說。「有一朵花……，我想她曾經馴養過我……。」

「這有可能，」狐狸說。「在地球上無奇不有。」

「哦！可是，這不是在地球上！」小王子說。

狐狸似乎很困惑，又很好奇。

「在別的星球上？」

「沒錯。」

「那個星球上有獵人嗎？」

「沒有。」

「啊！真是太棒了！有雞嗎？」

「沒有。」

「天下沒有十全十美的事。」狐狸嘆道。

不過，牠很快又回到正題。

「我的生活很單調，」牠說。「我獵雞吃，人們獵我。所有的雞都一個模樣，所有的人也是。因此，我感到有些厭煩。但是，如果你馴養我，我的生命便有如陽光照耀般地充滿光彩。我就會辨認出那種與眾不同的腳步聲。別的腳步聲會讓我嚇得趕緊躲到地下，你的腳步聲卻會像音樂一般地，把我從洞穴裡叫喚出來。然後你看，你看到下面那邊的麥田了嗎？我不吃麵包，小麥對我沒有什麼用處。麥田對我一點意義也沒有，這是很可悲的。可是，你有金黃色的頭髮，想想看，當你馴養我以後，那會是多麼美好的一件事！麥田的顏色也是金黃色的，這會讓我想起你。同時，我也會愛上聆聽風吹過麥田的聲音……。」

狐狸注視著小王子好一段時間。

「請你——馴養我吧！」牠說。

「我願意，非常願意，」小王子回答說。「可是，我的時間不多。我還要去找朋友，認識與瞭解許許多多的事情。」

「一個人只會瞭解他所馴養的東西，」狐狸說。「人們一向沒有太多的時間去瞭解任何事情。他們在商店裡買到所有現成的東西，但是在任何地方都找不到一個可以買到友誼的商店，所以人們也不再有朋友了。如果你想要一個朋友，就馴養我吧……。」

「要馴養你，我得做些什麼呢？」小王子問。

「你要很有耐心，」狐狸答道。「首先，你要坐在草地上離我不遠的地方——就像那樣。我會用眼角看著你，而你什麼話也不用說。語言是誤會的淵藪。但是，你每天要坐得更靠近我一點……」

隔天，小王子回來了。

「你最好每次回來的時間都一樣，」狐狸說。「舉例來說，假如你在下午四點回來，那麼，在三點的時候我就會開始高興了，時間越接近，我就越高興。到四點的時候，我便開始坐立不安，你不難發現我有多高興你的到來！但，如果你每次來的時間都不一樣，我便無法

假如你在下午四點回來，那麼，
在三點的時候我就會開始高興了。

得知要在什麼時候做好迎接你的心理準備……。人應該
遵守適當的儀式……。」

「什麼是儀式？」小王子問。

「那些也是常常被忽略的行為。」狐狸說道。「它
們會讓某一天不同於別的日子，某個小時不同於別的
時刻。例如，在獵人們就有一個儀式。每個星期四，他
們會跟村裡的女孩們跳舞。因此，星期四對我來說，就
是一個美好的日子，我可以一直散步到葡萄園去！但，
如果獵人們任何時間都可以跳舞，那麼，每天就跟所有
其他的日子沒有什麼不同，我便永遠不會有什麼假期
了。」

因此，小王子馴養了狐狸。當他離開的時刻即將到
來——

「啊，」狐狸說：「我會哭的。」

「這是你的錯，」小王子說。「我從未想過要傷害
你；但是你要我馴養你……。」

「是這樣沒錯。」狐狸說。

「可是，現在你卻想哭！」小王子說道。

「是啊，是這樣沒錯。」狐狸說。

「那麼，馴養你對你一點好處也沒有嘛！」

「當然有好處，」狐狸說：「因為麥田的顏色。」牠接著又說道：

　　「再去看看那些玫瑰花，你就會瞭解，你那朵玫瑰花是全世界獨一無二的。然後再回來跟我道別，我會送你一個祕密當作禮物。」

　　於是小王子走開，再去看看那些玫瑰花。

　　「妳們和我的玫瑰花一點也不像。」他說。「妳們仍是無足輕重的東西。因為沒有人曾馴養過妳們，妳們也未曾馴養過任何人。妳們就像我初次見到的那隻狐狸一般，牠不過就是其他成千上萬隻狐狸中的一隻。但是我和牠做了朋友，因此現在牠是全世界獨一無二的了。」

　　那些玫瑰花們覺得非常難為情。

　　「妳們是很美，不過也很空虛。」他繼續道：「沒有人會為妳們而死。當然，一般的路人會認為我的玫瑰花──那朵屬於我的玫瑰花，和妳們沒什麼兩樣，但對我而言，她比起妳們其他這幾百枝的玫瑰花來還要珍貴許多：因為我曾為她澆水；因為我曾把她放在玻璃罩下；因為我曾為她遮屏風；因為我曾為了她弄死了毛毛蟲（只留下兩、三隻來變成蝴蝶）；因為我曾傾聽她發

牢騷、自吹自擂，有時甚至只是沉默不語。因為她是我的玫瑰花。」

他又回到狐狸那裡。

「再見。」他說。

「再見，」狐狸說道。「這就是我的祕密，一個很簡單的祕密：只有用心靈才能把事情看得真確；重要的東西用肉眼是看不見的。」

「重要的東西用肉眼是看不見的。」小王子重複地說道，希望能把它牢牢記住。

「你為你的玫瑰花所花的時間，讓她變得那麼重要。」

「我為我的玫瑰花所花的時間——」小王子說道，如此他好確定已經記下了。

「人們早已忘了這個真理，但是你不可以忘記。你要永遠為你所馴養的東西負責，你要為你的玫瑰花負責……。」狐狸說。

「我要為我的玫瑰花負責，」小王子重複道，如此他好確定已經記下了。

22 🪐

🎧49

「早安。」小王子說。

「早安。」鐵路的扳閘員說。

「你在這裡做什麼?」小王子問道。

「我把旅客分類,一千個人一批,」扳閘員說:「然後把載運他們的火車送出去:有時往右,有時往左。」

一列燈火輝煌的快車,像雷鳴般轟隆地急馳而過,把扳閘員的小屋震得嘎嘎響。

「他們好匆忙啊,他們在找什麼呢?」小王子說。

「就連火車司機自己也不知道。」扳閘員說。

又有一列燈火通明的快車,往相反的方向轟隆隆地急馳而過。

「他們已經回來了嗎?」小王子問道。

「這不是剛剛的那些人,」扳閘員說。「這是一種交流。」

「他們不滿意原來的地方嗎?」小王子問。

「沒有人會滿意自己原來的所在。」扳閘員說。

他們又聽到第三列燈火明亮的快車狂嘯而過。

「他們在追趕第一批的旅客嗎？」小王子問。

「他們沒有在追趕什麼，」扳閘員說。「他們在裡面睡覺，如果沒有睡著，就是在打呵欠。只有小孩子們才會把鼻子壓靠在玻璃窗上往外看。」

「只有小孩子們知道他們在找什麼，」小王子說。「他們把時間花在一隻碎布娃娃上，那隻娃娃對他們來說就變得重要；如果有人把娃娃從他們身邊拿走，他們就會哭……。」

「他們很幸福。」扳閘員說。

23

「早安。」小王子說。

「早安。」商人說。

這是一位販售止渴藥丸的商人。只要一個星期服用一顆藥丸，你就不會感到口渴想喝東西了。

「你為什麼要賣那些藥丸呢？」小王子問。

「因為它們可以節省很多時間。」商人說。「專家們已經計算過，服用這種藥丸，你每個星期可以省下五十三分鐘。」

「省下的五十三分鐘，我要做些什麼呢？」

「做任何你想做的事……」

「就我而言，」小王子自語道：「假如我有五十三分鐘可以任意使用，我會從容地走向一處清涼的泉水。」

24 🪐

　　現在是我的飛機在沙漠裡失事的第八天。當我聽著商人的故事時，我正好喝下水壺裏的最後一滴水。

　　「啊！」我對小王子說：「你這些往事的內容很吸引人，可是我還沒有把飛機修理好，也沒有水可以喝了。如果我也可以從容地走向一處清涼的泉水，我會非常地高興！」

　　「我的狐狸朋友……。」小王子對我說。

　　「我親愛的小朋友，這件事與狐狸扯不上任何關係呀！」

　　「為什麼沒有關係？」

　　「因為我就快要渴死了……。」

　　他並沒有聽懂我的話，因為他回答說：

　　「即使快死了，能有個朋友也是件好事。譬如說，我就很高興能有狐狸這個朋友……。」

　　「他根本沒辦法猜想到現在的險況，」我自忖道。「他從未曾有過飢渴的感受。他所需要的可能只是一點點的陽光……。」

但他凝視著我，並對我心裡的想法答道：

「我也渴了。我們去找水井吧⋯⋯。」

我做了個感到厭煩的表情。在一望無際的沙漠中，漫無目的地找水井，實在荒謬可笑。但儘管如此，我們還是出發了。

當我們靜靜地跋涉幾個小時後，夜色臨至，群星開始露臉。我已經口乾舌燥得有些發燒，看著星星，宛如置身夢境一般。小王子最後所說的話，又浮現在我的腦海中：

「這麼說，你也會口渴？」我問道。

他沒有回答我的問題，只是對我說：

「水對於心靈或許也是有益的⋯⋯。」

我並不瞭解這些話的意思，不過我什麼也沒說。我很清楚，想要盤問他是不可能的事。

他累了，並坐了下來。我坐在他的身旁。沉默了一會之後，他又說道：

「這些星星真漂亮——因為一朵看不到的花的緣故。」

我答道：「對，的確如此。」之後，我沒有再說什麼，只靜靜地看著眼前在月光下向外延伸的沙脊。

「沙漠好美。」小王子又說。

這倒是真的。我一直都很喜歡沙漠。坐在沙漠的沙丘上，什麼也看不到，什麼也聽不見。然而，在一片靜寂之中，卻有個東西在跳動，在發光……。

「讓沙漠美麗的，」小王子說，「就是隱藏在某處的水井……。」

我突然醒悟那神祕的亮光為何物，心中驚訝不已。當我還是個小男孩時，曾住在一棟古屋中，據傳言裡面埋有寶藏。當然，從來沒有人知道該如何去尋找它；或許，從來也沒有人找過。但是，它卻為這棟房子投注了一股令人神往的氛圍。在我房子的中心深處，埋藏著一個祕密……。

「沒錯，」我對小王子說：「讓房子、星星或沙漠美麗的，就是某種看不見的東西！」

「我很高興，你同意我的狐狸所說的話。」他說。

當小王子睡著的時候，我把他抱入懷中，再度出發上路。我深受感動和興奮，彷彿我所懷抱的是一件非常脆弱的珍寶。我甚至覺得，在整個地球上再也找不到比他更脆弱的東西了。在月光下，我看著他蒼白的前額、緊閉的雙眼，以及在風中飄蕩的鬙髮。我忖道：

「我所看見的不過是副軀殼，最重要的是那些看不見的⋯⋯。」

　　他微張的嘴唇浮現出一絲笑意。我不禁又想：「這個熟睡中的小王子，讓我深受感動的，就是他對一朵花的忠誠──甚至在他睡著的時候，那朵玫瑰花的影像，就像一盞燈的光焰照耀著他全身⋯⋯。」於是，我覺得他彷彿變得更脆弱了。我覺得自己有必要保護他，因為他脆弱得好似一陣微風便能將之吹熄的火燄⋯⋯。

　　就這樣不停地走著，終於在破曉時分，我找到了一口水井。

25

「人們，」小王子說：「坐著快車出發，卻不知道他們在尋找什麼。接著他們便匆忙起來，變得興奮，不停地轉來轉去……。」

接著又說道：

「這麼做實在毫無意義……。」

我們找到的這口井，不像撒哈拉沙漠裡的水井。撒哈拉沙漠裡的水井僅是簡單地在沙地中挖洞罷了。這口井卻像鄉村裡的井，可是這裡沒有村莊，我想我一定是在作夢……。

「真奇怪，」我對小王子說。「每樣東西都準備妥當了：轆轤、水桶、繩索……。」

他笑著，拉住繩子，轉動轆轤。轆轤像個被風遺忘已久的古老風向標，發出嗚咽的悲泣聲。

「你聽到了嗎？」小王子問。「我們把井給叫醒了，它正唱著歌……。」

我不希望他因為拉繩子而把自己給累著了。

「讓我來吧，」我說。「這對你來說太重了。」

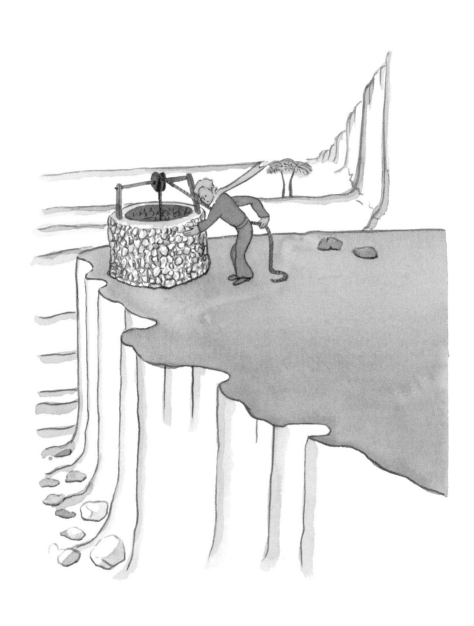

他笑著，拉住繩子，轉動轆轤。

　　我把水桶慢慢地拉放到井邊——雖然很累，但已經被成功的喜悅蓋過。耳中仍響著轆轤的歌聲，而且可以看見陽光在依舊晃動的水面上閃爍。

　　「我好想喝這些水，」小王子說：「給我一些水喝……。」

　　我終於瞭解他一直在尋找的是什麼東西。

　　我把水桶舉高到他的嘴邊。他閉上雙眼喝著水，彷彿甜美得有如節慶的饗宴一般。這些水也的確不同於其他一般的食物。它的甜美是來自於星夜下的跋涉、轆轤的歌唱和我雙手的勞動。它就像是一件對心靈有益的禮物。當我還是個小男孩時，聖誕樹上的燈光、午夜彌撒的音樂、溫柔的笑臉，常交織成我收到禮物時的光彩。

　　「住在這裡的人們，」小王子說：「在同一座花園裡栽種了五千朵玫瑰花——卻無法在那裡找到他們想要尋找的東西。」

　　「他們找不到。」我回答道。

　　「但他們所尋找的，卻有可能在一朵玫瑰花，或一小滴水中找到。」

　　「沒錯，這是事實。」我說。

　　小王子又接著道：

「眼睛是盲目的，人要用心靈來看……。」

喝過水後，我的呼吸順暢多了。日出時，沙漠呈現出一片蜂蜜的顏色，這種蜜色也讓我有快樂的感覺。那麼，是什麼讓我有悲傷的感覺呢？

「你得遵守你的諾言。」當小王子再次坐在我身旁時，他輕輕地說。

「什麼諾言？」

「你知道的——給我的綿羊畫一個口套……。我對我的花有責任……。」

我把我畫的草圖從口袋裡拿出來，小王子看過了以後，笑著說：

「你的猢猻麵包樹——看起來有點像包心菜。」

「啊！」

我還曾對我的猢猻麵包樹感到十分得意呢！

「你的狐狸——牠的耳朵看起來有點像牛角；而且太長了。」

他又笑了起來。

「你不公平，小王子，除了畫過看得見大蟒蛇的內部和看不見內部的圖外，我不會畫別的東西。」我說。

「噢，那不要緊，」他說：「小孩子看得懂。」

　　於是，我用鉛筆畫了一副口套，當我拿給他時，心裡非常難過、不捨。

　　「你有一些計畫，不知道是什麼。」我說。

　　不過，他沒有回答我，反而對我說：

　　「你知道的——我來到地球……。明天就是一周年了。」

　　接著，沉默了一會，他繼續說：

　　「我降落的地方離這裡很近。」

　　他臉紅了。

　　又一次，不知為何，我有一種古怪的哀傷感。不過，有個問題突然從我的腦海裡蹦出來：

　　「那麼，一個星期前，我第一次見到你的那天早上，不是偶然遇到的囉？當時，距離人煙千里以外的地方，你正獨自漫步。你是正朝著降落的地方往回走嗎？」

　　小王子的臉又紅了。

　　有點躊躇地，我又說：

　　「或許，是為了一週年的緣故？」

　　小王子再一次臉紅。他從不回答問題——但是，當一個人臉紅的時候，那不是意味著「是」嗎？

「哦，」我對他說：「我有點擔心……。」

　但是他打斷我的話。

　「現在你得工作。你要回去修理引擎，我會在這裡等你，你明天晚上再回來……。」

　可是我不放心。我想起了那隻狐狸，一個人一旦讓自己被人馴養後，就得承擔一點哭泣的風險……。

26

　　在水井旁，有一堵頹廢的老石牆。第二天晚上，當我做完工作再回來時，遠遠地我便看到小王子坐在石牆上，兩腳懸空晃動著，同時聽到他說：

　　「難道你忘了，這裡不是正確的地點。」

　　另外一個聲音一定有回覆他，因為我聽到他答道：

　　「是的，沒錯！就是這一天，不過，不是在這個地方。」

　　我繼續朝石牆走去，可是卻沒有看到任何人，或聽到任何人在說話。然而，小王子又回答：

　　「——沒錯。你會在沙地裡看到我足跡開始的地方，你只要在那裡等我就可以了。我今天晚上會在那裡。」

　　我距離石牆只有二十公尺遠，但仍然什麼也沒看到。

　　沉默了一會之後，小王子又說：

　　「你有劇毒嗎？你確定它不會讓我痛苦太久？」

　　我停下腳步，心裡一陣撕痛；可是，我仍然不明白這是怎麼一回事。

「現在走開吧，」小王子說。「我要從牆上下來了。」

我低頭往牆腳下一看——我嚇得跳起來。在我面前，面對著小王子的是一條在三十秒內就可以致人於死的黃蛇。即使當我從口袋裡拔出我的左輪手槍時，仍不免往後猛退一步。但是一聽到我發出的聲響，這條蛇便像快消失的噴水池水花一般從沙地上輕易溜走，並且發出輕微的金屬聲，不疾不徐地，隱沒在石頭堆中。

我抵達牆邊時，正好及時接住我的小朋友；他的臉色慘白如雪。

「這究竟是怎麼一回事？你為什麼在跟一條蛇講話？」我問道。

我把他一直戴著的金黃色圍巾鬆開，潤濕他兩邊的太陽穴，並讓他喝了些水。現在我不敢再問他更多問題，他神情十分嚴肅地望著我，還把兩手圈住我的脖子。我感覺到他的心跳，就像一隻被來福槍擊中垂死的小鳥一般……。

「我很高興你已經找出引擎的毛病出在哪裡了，現在你可以回家了……。」他說。

「你是怎麼知道的？」

現在走開吧，
我要從牆上下來了。

我正是要來告訴他，我的飛機已經修理好了，這是原先我不敢奢望的。

　　他沒有回答我的問題，不過他繼續說：

　　「我今天也要回家了⋯⋯。」

　　然後，他悲傷地說：

　　「那路途更遠⋯⋯。也更艱難⋯⋯。」

　　我清楚地瞭解到有什麼不尋常的事情發生了。我像擁著小嬰孩似的，把他緊緊地抱在懷裡；然而，就我看來，他彷彿正急速衝向一處深淵，而我卻無能為力⋯⋯。

　　他表情凝重，像個在遠方迷途的人。

　　「我有你給我的綿羊。我有綿羊的箱子。我還有口套⋯⋯。」

　　然後，他給我一個悽然的微笑。

　　等了好一段時間，我看得出來他正一點一滴的甦醒過來。

　　「親愛的小傢伙，你在害怕⋯⋯。」我對他說。

　　他在害怕，這是無庸置疑的。但是他卻輕輕地笑了起來。

　　「今天晚上我應該會更害怕⋯⋯。」

　　又一次，我感到自己因某種無法挽回的感覺而全身冰冷。我更清楚地知道，只要想到今後再也不能聽到這笑聲，便幾乎無法忍受。對我來說，這笑聲就有如沙漠中的一脈清泉。

　　「小傢伙，」我說，「我想再聽聽你的笑聲。」

　　但是他對我說：

　　「今晚，就要一年了……。這樣，我的星星就可以在一年前我來到地球之處的正上方找到……。」

　　「小傢伙，」我說，「告訴我，這有關蛇、會面的地方，還有星星的事——都只是一場惡夢……。」

　　但他沒有回應我的懇求。相反地，他對我說：

　　「重要的事情肉眼是看不見的……。」

　　「是的，我知道……。」

　　「它就和那朵花一樣。如果你愛一朵長在某顆星星上的花，那麼，在夜晚仰望星空是一件很甜美的事。所有的星星都盛開著花……。」

　　「是啊，我知道……。」

　　「它就和這水一樣。因為那轆轤、繩索，所以你給我喝的水就像音樂一樣美妙。你記得嗎——它是多麼地甘甜啊。」

「我當然記得……」

「在夜晚你會仰望星空。我住的地方,每樣東西都太小了,所以我沒有辦法指給你看我的星球在哪裡。其實,這樣也好。對你來說,我的星球會是那些星星中的一顆。為此,你會喜愛去觀看天上所有的星星……。它們都會成為你的朋友。另外,我還要送你一份禮物……。」

他又笑了起來。

「啊,小王子,親愛的小王子!我好喜歡聽到這個笑聲!」

「那就是我的禮物。就這樣。它就像我們喝水時……。」

「你想說什麼?」

「每個人都擁有星星,」他回答:「但是對不同的人,它們有不同的意義。對旅行者而言,它們是嚮導。對其他人而言,它們也不過是天空中的小亮光罷了。對學者而言,它們是道難題。對我的商人朋友來說,它們便是財富。不過所有的星星都是緘默的。你——唯有你——所擁有的星星與其他人都不同……。」

「你究竟想說什麼?」

「我就住在這些星星裡其中的一顆，我會在那上面笑著。因此，當你仰望星空時，就好像所有的星星都在笑著……。你——唯有你——能擁有會笑的星星！」

然後，他又笑了起來。

「還有，當你的哀傷得到慰藉時（時間會撫平所有的哀傷），你就會因為曾認識我而感到滿足。你將會永遠成為我的朋友，想要同我一起歡笑。因此，為了那種快樂，有時你會打開窗戶……。當你的朋友看到你對著天空大笑時，一定會感到很驚訝！那時，你就會對他們說：『沒錯，星星常會令我大笑！』那麼，他們就會認為你瘋了。這將會是我跟你開的一個大玩笑……。」

他又笑了。

「那就好像我給你的不是星星，而是許多會笑的小鈴鐺……。」

他再次笑了起來。然後他馬上又嚴肅地說：

「今天晚上——你知道的……。不要來。」

「我不要離開你。」我說。

「我會看起來好像很痛苦，我會看起來好像快死掉似的。大概就是像那種樣子。不要來看，不值得這麼麻煩……。」

「我不要離開你。」

但是他擔心了。

「我告訴你——那也是因為那條蛇的緣故。你絕對不能被牠咬到。蛇——是很惡毒的生物。這條蛇有可能只是為了好玩而咬你⋯⋯。」

「我不要離開你。」

不過，轉念一想，他就安心了：

「那倒是事實——牠們沒有多餘的毒液可以咬第二口。」

那天晚上我沒有看到他動身出發，他無聲無息地離開我。當我終於趕上他時，他正以快速且毅然決然的步伐走著。他僅只對我說：

「啊！你來了⋯⋯。」

他牽著我的手，但仍然感到憂心。

「你不應該來的。你會很難受，因為我看起來會像死了似的；不過那不是真的⋯⋯。」

我沉默不語。

「你知道的⋯⋯。路太遠了，我沒辦法帶著這個軀殼一起走。它太重了。」

我默不作聲。

　　「不過它會像一個被遺棄的舊軀殼一樣，一副舊軀殼沒有什麼好悲傷的……。」

　　我依然靜默。

　　他有些氣餒，但依舊再次努力地說：

　　「你知道，這會是很美好的。我也會仰望著星星，所有的星星上面都會有生了銹的轆轤水井，所有的星星都會傾瀉出清新的水供我喝……。」

　　我仍舊不語。

　　「那多有趣啊！你會有五億個小鈴鐺，而我則會有五億個清新的泉水……。」

接著，他也不再作聲，因為他哭了……。

「就是這裡。讓我自個過去吧。」

他坐了下來，因為他在害怕。然後他又說道：

「你知道的——我的花……。我得對她負責。她是那麼的嬌弱！那麼的天真！她僅有四根一點也派不上用場的刺，來保護她抵禦這個世界……。」

我也坐了下來，因為我再也站不住了。

「好了——就這樣了……。」

他仍有些猶豫；隨即他站了起來。他邁開了一步，我卻無法動彈。

除了在他的腳踝附近有一道黃色的閃光外，那裡什麼也沒有。有一刻，他一動也不動。沒有叫喊出聲，他像一棵樹般地緩緩倒下。因為是在沙地上的緣故，甚至連一絲聲響也沒有。

他坐了下來，
因為他在害怕。

27

🎧 54

迄今已經六年過去了……我從未曾向人說過這個故事。迎接我歸來的朋友都很高興見到我仍活著。但我很悲傷，不過我告訴他們說：「我累了。」

如今，我的悲傷已經得到一些紓緩。也就是說——不是完全紓解。但是我知道，他確實已經回到他的星球了，因為在天亮的時候，我找不到他的身體。他的身體其實沒那麼重……。夜晚時，我喜歡傾聽星星的聲音，那就像五億個小鈴鐺……。

可是有一件很特別的事情……當我幫小王子畫口套的時候，忘了把皮帶加上去，所以，很可能他永遠都沒有辦法用它套住羊的嘴巴。因此，現在我會不停地想道：他的星球現在怎樣了？或許，羊已經把花給吃了……。

有時我會對自己說：「一定不會的！小王子每天晚上都會把花放在玻璃罩裡，而且他非常小心地看守著他的綿羊……。」這時，我就會覺得很快樂，所有的星星也都笑得很甜美。

他像一棵樹般地緩緩倒下，
連一絲聲響也沒有……

可是，有時我又會對自己說：「人難免都會有疏忽的時候，而一次也就夠了！若是某個晚上他忘了把花放進玻璃罩內，或是那隻綿羊在夜裡悄無聲息地偷跑出來……。」這時，這些小鈴鐺就變成了一顆顆的淚珠……。

　　這是一件非常神祕的事。對於也愛小王子的你──還有我──來說，整個宇宙將會完全改觀：如果在我們所不知的某個地方，一隻我們從來未曾見過的羊，已經──或者沒有──吃了一朵玫瑰花……。

　　仰望天空，問問你自己：是有，還是沒有呢？羊已經把花吃了嗎？那麼，你就會領悟所有的東西都已不復以往……。

　　沒有一個大人能夠瞭解，這是一件多麼重要的事！

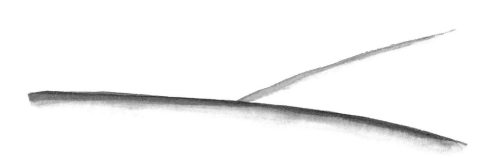

對我來說，這是世上最美也最哀傷的景色。它和前一頁的景色一樣，但是我把它再畫了一次，以加深你的記憶。就是在這裡，小王子在地球上出現，又消失了。

　　仔細地看這幅圖畫，以便哪天你到非洲沙漠去旅行時，可以確認出來。再者，假如你經過這個地方，請不要匆匆而過。請你在這顆星星的正下方等一會，如果有一位面帶微笑，有著金黃色的頭髮，而且不回答問題的小傢伙出現的話，那麼，你就知道他是誰了。如果有發生這種事，請你捎個信息來撫慰我，讓我知道他已經回來了。

The Little Prince
小王子

MP3
寂天雲 APP
或登入官網下載音檔
www.icosmos.com.tw

作者 ｜ 安東尼・聖艾修伯里（Antoine de Saint-Exupéry）

譯者 ｜ 李思

出版 ｜ 寂天文化事業股份有限公司

發行人 ｜ 黃朝萍

封面/內頁設計 ｜ 林書玉

電話 ｜ 02-2365-9739

傳真 ｜ 02-2365-9835

網址 ｜ http://www.icosmos.com.tw

E-mail ｜ onlineservice@icosmos.com.tw

郵撥帳號 ｜ 1998620-0
寂天文化事業股份有限公司

出版日期 ｜ 2024年02月　初版再刷【英漢典藏版】（寂天雲隨身聽APP版）(0102)

・訂書金額未滿1000元，請外加運費100元。若有破損，請寄回更換。

小王子 (寂天雲隨身聽APP版) / 安東尼・聖艾修伯里（Antoine de Saint-Exupéry）著；李思譯. —初版. —[臺北市]：寂天文化事業股份有限公司, 2022.12印刷　面；公分.
英漢典藏版＋中英情境故事有聲書譯自: The little prince
ISBN 978-626-300-172-5　(25K精裝)
1.CST: 英語 2.CST: 讀本　876.57　111019583

You become responsible, forever, for what you have tamed.
You are responsible for your rose…

If someone loves a flower, of which just one single blossom grows in all the millions and millions of stars, it is enough to make him happy just to look at the stars.